Praise for *The Precariousness of Done*

"*The Precariousness of Done* is a powerful work: a moving, courageous and daring narration of the difficulties of a person with obsessive-compulsive disorder. A valuable and enriching contribution to the struggle against the stigma that millions of anonymous sufferers heroically, resiliently and secretly battle to overcome."

> —Pedro Martín-Barrajón Morán, Director of Crisis and Emergency Management PSYA SPAIN, S.L.
> Also: Psychologist, General Coordinator of the National Network of Emergency Psychologists in Railway Accidents. MS in Clinical Psychology and Health. MS in Suicidal Behaviors. University Specialist in Post-Traumatic Stress Disorder (PTSD)

"*The Precariousness of Done* es una obra impactante: conmovedora, valiente y atrevida por narrar las dificultades de una persona con trastorno obsesivo-compulsivo. Una valiosa y enriquecedora contribución a la lucha contra el estigma que millones de luchadores anónimos combaten de manera heroica, resiliente y clandestina por superar."

> —Pedro Martín-Barrajón Morán, Director Gestión de Crisis y Emergencias PSYA SPAIN, S.L.
> También: Psicólogo, Coordinador General Red Nacional Psicólogos de Emergencias en Accidentes Ferroviarios. Máster Psicología Clínica y Salud. Máster Conductas Suicidas. Especialista universitario en Trastorno de Estrés Postraumático (PTSD)

More praise for *The Precariousness of Done*

"Houck paints a vivid Spanish backdrop for a complex entanglement of characters whose stories are rich with suspense and longing. Both emotionally haunting and full of heart, *The Precariousness of Done* is a strong debut from a writer who knows how to twist his way through a tale."

—Greg Shemkovitz, author of *Lot Boy*

"In *The Precariousness of Done*, Houck has without a doubt created a captivating story of depth that leaves the reader reflecting on the fear that drives our desire to protect ourselves and others. Each of us can relate to the sometimes hindering and sometimes motivating influence our own personal fears have on our path in life."

—Meg McSherry, LCSW, Courage Health & Wellness, Fredericksburg, VA

The PRECARIOUSNESS of DONE

The PRECARIOUSNESS of
DONE

TONY HOUCK

Brandylane
Publishers, Inc.
Publishing books since 1985

ISBN: 978-1-947860-14-8
LCCN: 2018959708

Designed by Michael Hardison
Production management by Robert H. Pruett

Printed in the United States of America

Published by Brandylane Publishers, Inc.
5 S. 1st Street
Richmond, Virginia 23219
brandylanepublishers.com | belleislebooks.com

Brandylane
Publishers, Inc.
Publishing books since 1985

To Jennifer and Noah

In the stillness of midnight,

                    as you twitch and drift off to sleep,

An overt and senseless urge compels

Me to relock and rattle our front door

                      —four times, always four—

Nudge the remote you set down "wrong" on the nightstand,

Or stand in the bedroom doorway,

                  anxiously scrutinizing the lifeless

Television set—"I know it's off," I whisper to

Myself but continue to stare irrationally,

              distracted by the light on the cable box.

You wake but do not sigh or huff or make any sound,

Only cracking your bleary eyes to look past my outward

Compulsions to see the person inside

                —a good and patient man who

Detests the behaviors he feels bound to engage in

            and who dedicates this book to you.

ACKNOWLEDGEMENTS

A debt of gratitude to Robert Pruett and everyone at Brandylane Publishers for their belief in first-time authors.

To my critical readers, Jane Gatewood, Catherine Ham, Adam Houck, Leissa Shahrak, and Greg Shemkovitz, for helping polish the manuscript without breaking my spirit.

For the gift of his time and extensive experience in marketing communications, Kip Smith, and for their advice on reaching my goal of getting published, Kristi Tuck Austin and James Warren.

I cannot fully express my gratitude to my exceptional high school teachers—Barbara Graves, Jackie Holt, Betsy Stulz, and David Webb.

To the friends who became family during my studies after high school in Las Rozas, Spain, especially Paloma Martín and her family, and Juan Antonio Tirado.

To my Spanish friend of twenty-five years, José Luis Ruiz, for educating me about *toros bravos* (brave bulls) and safely guiding me as I ran with them, and for his steadfastness from across the pond.

And finally, in a novel that draws so heavily on my severe obsessive-compulsive disorder, I must mention those who encourage, support, and tolerate this imperfect man on a daily basis—my wife, Jennifer, and our son, Noah.

"The brain is a battlefield where we trade victories and losses with ourselves."

—Sandra Clemens

PROLOGUE

Las Rozas, Spain

March 1996

"Eres un subnormal profundo—You are a profound retard."

Thehe insult had burst through Ethan's door just minutes into the new year, as he lay propped against his pillow, ingesting the Spanish edition of Ernest Hemingway's *The Old Man and the Sea*. The abuse had cut the eighteen-year-old, but it had not surprised him, despite his host mother's resolution to "be more maternal." He had given her an archaic smile and gone back to reading.

But now, three months after slumping into bed with an old fisherman at twenty-two past midnight—for Spain, quite early but not *retardedly* so—Ethan wasn't smiling. Anxious, the bright yet painfully shy teenager perched on the side of the bed.

The bunk was designed to save space: a bookcase wall bed—the convenience of a twin Murphy bed, the storage of side cabinets with adjustable shelves. The unit had been a closeout, and it rocked slightly. Thankfully, it had never fallen on anyone, but no one had ever gotten a restful night's sleep on the "mattress" either. Ethan didn't blame his host parents for the miserable thing, tucking him into their house-rich, cash-poor lives however they could. Nevertheless, the room was a bedroom in name only.

It was the tiniest space in a suite of rooms with parquet floors and stark white walls that occupied part of what Spaniards call the second floor but Americans call the third floor of the latest housing development. Regardless of the floor numbering scheme used inside the building, its anemic red brick exterior lacked style and grace.

A walkway led from the buzz-in entrance through pea green grass watered and mined by Chihuahuas and a German shepherd, and then pierced a short wall separating the private lawn from the public sidewalk. The pedestrian-friendly street was typical of those in the burgeoning yet walkable town of Las Rozas. The name meant "clearings," and though its origin was unclear (likely agricultural, as *roza* in Castilian refers to a place cleared for farmland), for Ethan, Las Rozas was home.

The exception was his host parents' apartment. It was the place where he disagreed most with the words of his exchange studies adviser: "Differences aren't good or bad, just different." She hadn't been referring to an acrimonious couple but to general cultural differences (female nudity on broadcast television, for example), and he had agreed with her, for the most part. And though dealing with an adopted culture wasn't always as pleasurable as watching a topless woman savor a spoonful of yogurt, Ethan did so like a trouper.

He was a child of natural parents who were quietly living married yet separate lives under the same roof, so he was ill-prepared for the *matrimonio*'s biting words to each other. Ethan persisted through, fearing that someone would end his studies prematurely.

Swallowing his complaints had done him little good, though. He sat back, heeling one of two large boxes his natural mother had shipped at great expense. God bless the woman for trying to buoy his withering waistline with non-perishable tastes of home: hot sauce, spray cheese, peanut butter, Triscuits, powdered milk.

Or on second thought, maybe the Almighty should impose a little penance on her for turning a deaf ear to Ethan's wish that she simply wire pesetas: "so many boxes" irritated his host mother, the caretaker of a Spartan kitchen with few cabinets. Where was he to put groceries in his postage stamp-sized quarters? Certainly not in plain sight, even if he stayed. And if he got the boot, he might simply trash them, although he hated the thought of tossing out good food almost as much as leaving.

Ethan tucked his hands underneath him and stared at his host father's mouth: Looking a person in the eyes was an ability that often eluded the introvert.

"What's clearer than water is that your behavior cannot continue," the man who ran the roost declared, arms crossed.

The walls closed in on Ethan. "I'm not sure what I've done wrong," he managed to say with a Castilian accent that would be perfect if he hung on until June.

"Not sure what you've done wrong?" the man asked, palming the greasy hair stuck to his scalp.

"Not really," Ethan said.

The man leaned back in his chair and laced his nicotine-stained fingers behind his head. "I find that hard to believe."

Ethan caught a whiff of body odor: Soccer had been on the *tele*, and his host father had forgone his bubbly, weekly preening.

Even the bathroom (tub shower, toilet, bidet—an odd fixture— vanity, linen closet) was larger than Ethan's bedroom. At night, when his window and its rackety shutter were closed because his host mother "said so," the room was claustrophobic. Only by the light leaking in under the door, which was also to remain shut, could he see the hand in front of his face.

"Or maybe," the man continued, "you're just too much of a *troglodita* to see it."

As a child of a marriage disintegrating two thousand miles away, it hadn't taken Ethan long to puzzle out his host mother's behavior: Standing up to the rooster who strutted around his barnyard was an ability that often eluded her, so she brooded and pecked at her host son. But her husband's demeanor had been apparent from the very start: Reveling in his own crowing, he was just an ecumenical cock.

"Never in my life have I seen such an odd young man," the old bird said.

Ethan stared at the floor, wondering if he would still have somewhere to perch come dawn. "If this is about the *Krispis* . . ."

His host father laughed at him. "This is about much more than cereal."

"I don't—"

"You weren't the only student we could have chosen, understand? Do you know what I'm telling you? There were other choices, but we chose *you*."

Ethan's slate blue eyes watched his wristwatch tick away the afternoon.

"Of all the teenagers in *Estados Unidos*, we chose the one who doesn't like cereal."

"I like cereal," Ethan assured him yet again; "what I don't like is the taste of the milk you buy."

"The milk tastes fine," the cock said.

"Brick milk is quite different from what I'm used to."

"What kind do you—" The man caught himself: "That's right; you drink milk that's sold in bottles."

Ethan nodded. "It's perishable but doesn't taste funny, at least to—"

"We don't buy that kind of milk," the cock declared. "Don't ask me again."

I didn't ask you before, Ethan wanted to insist.

"*We* don't eat Krispis. I bought and paid for them for *you*."

Ethan had little doubt that his host mother had actually done the shopping. Besides, they were compensated for his day-to-day expenses. "If I had known the Krispis were so important to you, I would have eaten them dry. I'll eat them dry."

"And could you check the gas bottle before you shower *every* day?"

Ethan couldn't believe the man was harping on the butane again. "I do check it," he said, "and I only forgot that one time . . . way back in September. I apologized—"

"But your apology didn't buy a full gas bottle, did it?"

Ethan felt like a puppy that had once piddled on the rug and was having his nose rubbed in the invisible stain.

"The wife couldn't make dinner; Burger King doesn't give away Whoppers and *patatas fritas*, understand? You're strange but smart. I know you know what I'm saying."

"I understand," Ethan said faintly, "and as I said before, my house in Bir-he-nia (Virginia) has pipe gas, not gas bottles. Without a gauge or a scale, it's hard to judge how much is left in one of those things."

"Didn't you pick it up?"

Ethan wanted to scream. "Again, it felt about half full."

"But it wasn't," the cock said wryly.

"No, it wasn't. Sorry."

Additional rebukes and apologies lasted until the door creaked open. A woman's voice ventured through the crack: "I'm going to mass."

Her husband wiped the saliva off the corner of his mouth. "Fine."

"And don't forget to have the late-afternoon snack, you two."

"Make it before you go," the cock said, "and I'll eat it later."

"I don't have time."

The man glanced at Ethan's watch. "It's only six fifteen, and mass doesn't start until seven o'clock. There's plenty of time."

"No, there isn't," the voice insisted.

The cock left oily fingerprints as he pushed back from the table. "Why not?" he asked, swaggering forward.

"Because I'm taking a sanity break."

The cock clutched the doorknob, his knuckles reddening. "So you have the time, but won't take the time."

"No . . . no, I won't."

"What about the *café*?"

"You'll have to make it."

"Why haven't you done it?"

"Because God frowns at sinners who are late to mass," his wife said. "There's *yogur* in the refrigerator, behind the milk."

Dispirited and hungry, Ethan began to push back his cuticles, tending to each finger in exactly the same way as he gazed out the window. Outside, the light was turning soft, but inside the mood was already hard. He rocked forward and watched his host mother retreat. "And there's cereal to go with that milk," he said, thoughtlessly trying to lighten the mood. Or maybe he knew exactly what he was doing.

The cock shoved the door open and chased after his hen. The two exchanged idle threats of divorce—nothing unusual—and then the front door thudded shut. The man locked and chained it, waltzed into the kitchen, and clanged together the makings of a small pot of coffee.

After cursing his cigarette lighter, he lit the burner with a match as gas flowed plentifully from the gas bottle on the balcony. Waiting for the water to boil, he opened a package of fairy cakes and ate one of the light, spongy cupcakes as he stood at the stove.

Minutes later, the aroma of stovetop coffee drifted on the silence. It was followed by the sporadic tings of a glass espresso cup settling into its saucer. Another fairy cake, a warmed cup of *café con leche*, the return of the opened brick of milk to the refrigerator, the rustle of a new pack of cigarettes. The cock strutted out of the kitchen.

Kneeling on the bed, Ethan banked the memory of the mountains to the north silhouetted a deep reddish-purple by the sunset. After four tugs on the belt built into the wall, he was insulated by the roller shutter from the hominess of Las Rozas. He turned to face the starkness of the situation.

The cock stood in the doorway, legs apart, hands on hips, a lit Marlboro pinched between his lips. "I have made my decision."

FRIDAY, 4 OCTOBER 2002

Las Rozas, Spain

16:00 h

The crisp but cozy kitchen was scented orange. Three halved fruits lay reamed on a plate, their rinds and pulp destined to be made into marmalade. Jars of mango-raspberry and pear-lemon were impeccably stacked in the cupboard. The widow enjoyed the preserves daily, serving them with cheese, folding them into whipped cream, spreading them on toast, or dolloping them onto cookies.

She softened the fourth orange—four per glass of juice, always four—cut it in two, and then knife-poked the seeds into the trash. The juicer's motor groaned as she pressed a half-fruit onto the reamer.

It's too dry, she told herself, staring at the nectar collecting in the glass. She lightly watered the reamer until pale juice flowed down the spout, and then collected some in a spoon. *Needs a little sugar*. A lime-colored sugar bowl with white polka dots, a clean spoon, rhythmic stirring.

For a moment, the even rhythm of the tings distracted her guest, a kindred spirit named Thomas. The widow often provided him refuge. He lingered at the banquette, sunk into a cushion color coordinated with the tableware. Struggling to ignore a persistent, intrusive thought, he dug his elbows into the tablecloth. Agnostic at best, he wondered if there was a God, why he had been dealt the card of obsessive-compulsive. He laced his fingers as if to pray, but the gesture was simply an attempt to endure the hiccups of a mental disorder. No amount of supplication would make a damned bit of difference.

He had almost folded once, lost in the rattling of a doorknob that some part of his brain wasn't sure was locked. But the dull blade he had snatched from his father's toolbox made suicide too painful for someone who wasn't sure he actually wanted to die. The faint scar was at times a badge of courage; at others, one of cowardice, but he was still playing the hand he had been given, the very best he knew how to, no longer so naïve as to believe that his best was good enough.

To cover the mark, he wore a bracelet: leather, braided, the ware of a street vendor during Las Rozas's annual *fiestas,* saint's day festival. A gift from his intimate Marisa.

She had tied the first band around his wrist and then cinched the knot, manicured it, and dabbed it with superglue to proof it against his obsession that it would loosen. For two years, the bracelet had twisted—"shit!"—and rolled out of place—"dammit!"—but Marisa's knot had never budged, even when the braiding became threadbare. Moments ago, she had yanked the shabby band off him and given him another, tying and tending to it as she had the first one.

But the cap on Marisa's old tube of glue was dead tight. Apologetic and self-critical, she had hurried off to the hardware store. Until the new bracelet was proofed against his obsession—if such a thing were even possible—he would be further plagued by anxiety and doubt. Another blip on his crowded mental radar.

He tugged at the knot, hoping that Marisa would return soon, and aware that what he was doing made no fucking sense. But he had, had, had, had to do it anyway.

The widow plated the last orange rind, nudging the eight halves into an octagon, and handed Thomas a glass.

"Here, drink this," she said with an aged voice in the southern dialect. The omission of consonants and vowels, even syllables, helped the words flow off her tongue. Although she pronounced certain *c*'s and *z*'s differently than the supposedly more "cultivated" Madrileños, she was as refined as any señora in Spain when it came to the things in life that really mattered.

"Thank you very much," Thomas stuttered, catching Mercedes's every word.

Her name meant "mercies"; Thomas had never met someone so aptly named . . .

She was Andalusian by birth, born in a speck of a house in need of a whitewash in a Republican town about a day's walk from Seville. She was berated as a child for obsessions and compulsions that slowed her chores, but her father's belt had not quickened her pace.

She had been sent to fetch rushes from the riverbank on the morning he was killed—rounded up by a Nationalist death squad, beaten with a rifle butt into digging a shallow hole, and shot for supporting the Republic.

The rat-a-tat sent Mercedes running into the fields, where she cowered until nightfall and slinked home past a mass grave.

Francisco Franco's fascist troops had taken the town; gangs of them had their way with the women to intimidate neighboring populations. Mercedes was untouched, her mother was not.

In total, the *Guerra Civil* lasted three years, from 1936 to 1939. Atrocities were committed by both sides; the grisliness of World War II's "dress rehearsal" shocked the world. Spain nearly bled to death.

Desperate to escape the hunger that followed *La Guerra*, Mercedes accepted a hasty proposal from the son of a herdless cattleman and married at fourteen with her mother's consent. Two months after the marriage, she finally gave herself to him.

They headed north, eking out an existence in the town of Pozoblanco on her flawless seams and pleats, and then in the village of Navahermosa on his strong back until the work dried up. After a famished stay in Toledo, he found steady work as a bricklayer in Las Rozas with the *Dirección General de Regiones Devastadas*, the organization in charge of postwar reconstruction. Most of the *Regiones* neighborhood bore his trowel marks, including the *piso*, apartment, in which Mercedes still lived.

Their only child was born in the kitchen and baptized in the church across the street.

Mercedes made most of the boy's clothes and walked him to school until she embarrassed him. Even then, they prepared and ate the midday *comida* together, unless he went home with a friend, something that happened more and more. His father taught him to make *paella valenciana*, a mélange of rice, chicken, rabbit, and beans: Paella is man's work.

He lived at home until he was thirty, working as a waiter to save for the day he met "the girl I'm going to marry." During a slow shift he did. Her adoptive parents paid for most of the wedding. The bride was a virgin and wore white.

Eleven months later, a driver who had an epileptic fit behind the wheel struck the young couple as they were crossing the street. They died instantly, but a new mother's panicked shove had sent her infant's carriage careening to safety, toward Mercedes, who was waiting at the curb.

As the sheets fell over the bodies, Mercedes became the mother of her grandchild Churro. He would eventually nickname her "*Ma-buelita*," a blend of the words "*mamá*—mom" and "*abuelita*—grandma*." He would call his grandpa "*Pa-buelito*."

Like the rushes Mercedes had gathered as a child, the new family bent but did not break. Pa-buelito returned to work the day after the funeral. His public face remained as hard as the bricks he laid, but in private he became as soft as unfired clay. Mercedes's obsessions and compulsions had always slowed her housework, and to her sweeping, dusting, cooking, and washing were added diapering, feeding, burping, and rocking. Her transition from grandmotherhood to motherhood was bumpy, but her devotion to Churro was unwavering. In time, Ma-buelita and Pa-buelito found their new normal.

Churro never really took to the powdered formula that Ma-buelita gave him, but the drone of the electric juicer sent him toddling into the kitchen. And sheep on the windmill-dotted plains of La Mancha had a hard time keeping up with his demand for Manchego cheese when he turned five.

He was a cautious boy who seemed to stretch rather than grow through an unremarkable childhood into adolescence. He was humble and honest, and spoke the truth in a gentle, almost matter-of-fact sort of way. Catholic by baptism, agnostic by choice, he read the Bible for inspiration and encyclopedias for information, and took his cues from nature.

He saw no point to most conversations about politics or religion, and when it came to the older generation's addiction to tradition, he was clean. Except for the bulls. They had been in his blood since Mercedes boosted him onto a stool to watch bullocks lead six of the snotty beasts down the street and part a throng of teenagers who were desperate to prove their manhood.

Despite her protests, he had become a novice bullfighter at the age of twenty. His lankness and long arms lent themselves to flowing lines with the capote, the magenta-and-yellow cape used during the early stages of a bullfight. But his trepid manner with the scarlet muleta and the sword made his performance clumsy. After years of mediocrity, no *matador de toros* had ever been patron to his joining the ranks. Age ensured that he would don his secondhand suit of lights only as an avocation.

Mercedes nearly wore the beads off her rosary (the first of two wedding gifts from her mother) each time Churro stepped onto that bloody dance floor. If his pas de deux with the bulls were nothing more than the amped pursuit of glory, her protests would have had teeth. But she knew he felt alive so close to death, a death that could have come when he was a baby riding in a carriage.

His birth mother's shove had saved him. "But why?" "What if it hadn't?" Mercedes's blind faith had given him an unsatisfactory answer to the first question; his pondering on the second one sent him into the bullring to battle the ghost he had not become.

Churro's next fight began within the hour . . .

Thomas finished the glass of orange juice Mercedes had given him and stared at the pulp scattered over the bottom of the glass. The soggy bits of fruit formed shapes and figures that could have been read like tea leaves. He scoffed at such things as fortunetelling and prophesying, but not Mercedes. Born and raised near Seville, the southern señora had a few drops of gypsy blood dancing through her veins. Thomas wondered if she had read Churro's fortune; the novice bullfighter had downed a glass of Ma-buelita's juice before leaving for the bullring.

Despite Thomas's scoffing at soothsaying and his uncertainty that Mercedes had even read Churro's pulpy fortune, a question about what she might have seen intruded itself into his thoughts: OCD thrust illogical, strange, and unwanted things into Thomas's head. Ignoring the intrusion caused him anxiety, but as his stare moved from the glass to the new bracelet, Mercedes interrupted.

"How do you feel?" she asked Thomas.

"A little better," he said and checked the clock. "We should probably get going." He tidied the tablecloth, left the chair as he had found it, and moved to the sink. "The walk will do us good."

Quietly reciting the Act of Contrition, Mercedes nodded.

Thomas rhythmically rinsed the glass as he watched the neighbor's clothesline: "There's not a breath of wind, so Churro's cape should behave."

"Yes," Mercedes whispered and mashed the weary snap of her purse.

Wind or not, the rosary beads were in for a long afternoon.

19:00 h

Across the street beside her father's ground-floor *taberna*, Ethan's surrogate sister and her fiancé watched a compact flirt with a parking space. Parallel parking on side streets in Las Rozas was a relative term, especially during the fiestas, when more wheels hopped the sidewalk than hugged the curb, so Rebeca and Álvaro waited to cross the street.

"Hold this," Rebeca said politely, handing her handbag to Álvaro, and wound a scrunchy around her ponytail as she eyed La Rinconera. Her father's modest yet popular bar also served food, and she was glad to see that the tables by the window were still full after the peak of the *merienda*, the late-afternoon snack that helped tide Spaniards over until the usual dinnertime of nine or ten o'clock. "I'm hungry," she said and patted her flat stomach.

Álvaro nodded and then peeked at the seat of Rebeca's jeans.

Ethan had lagged behind, walking with María Luisa, the other daughter of the family who had taken him under its wing during his exchange stay. Without their care, he never would have survived those final months.

María Luisa frowned as Rebeca rebuffed the hand Álvaro slipped into her back pocket. Papá would not approve, but she would say nothing.

Sr. Serrano's daughters were disappointments to him; María Luisa, the older of the two, even more so. Pushing thirty, she lived at home, attended classes sporadically, and wanted no part of the taberna, except for the perks of being the boss's daughter.

In conversation, he attributed her aimlessness to a culture whose doting on its children enabled millions of Peter Pans, but deep inside he had always felt that she could sense the blame he tacitly cast on her for the Reye's Syndrome that had taken his baby son, Félix. The rare but potentially fatal disease of the brain and liver was associated with a viral infection, but she had been just a little girl with the chicken pox. More than twenty years later, María Luisa could count on one hand the number of productive conversations she had had with her father.

Moderately depressed, she had put on considerable weight since Ethan's exchange stay, but his hugs were no less firm. Her father had no patience for mental disorders, but he realized the upside of his daughter's souring and growing disposition: Men weren't knocking on the door of her self-imposed cloister, tempting her to break his cardinal rule of dating. Alone in her bedroom, it was up to God if she didn't keep things above the waist.

As sweet as her sister was thick, Rebeca presented a different set of challenges.

She was a good girl who had never given her parents real cause for concern during her two serious relationships: Hermán, serving compulsory military service, had been absent during Ethan's entire exchange stay; Álvaro, a hobbyist and waiter in the employ of Sr. Serrano, was ever present.

But the apple of Sr. Serrano's eye had lost her shine. He had supported her dreams (hiking guide, photographer, youth counselor, to name a few), but his money hadn't cured her aimlessness. And though she wasn't opposed to hard work, she didn't seem eager to try it.

She had settled on homemaker, not the most ambitious undertaking, considering her intention to delay having children until she and Álvaro got settled. But she would be out from under his roof come summer.

Sr. Serrano was going to miss her, but not that mouth of hers. It never stopped. Well, almost never. There was that afternoon they had discovered little Rebeca was severely allergic to *guindilla* peppers. Since then, Sra. Navas—a Spanish woman's first surname remains the same after marriage—made two versions of *pisto*, a stew of peppers, zucchini, and onion in fried tomato sauce.

Whether she made it with guindillas or green peppers, Ethan wolfed it down. She had taught him to make it during his exchange stay, on one of the many nights Rebeca or María Luisa had invited him to dinner. Home alone, tired of Whoppers and *patatas fritas*, feeling like his host parents' not-so-new puppy, Ethan had rarely refused the girls' offers.

When, standing in Ethan's bedroom with a lit Marlboro bouncing between his lips, Ethan's cock of a host father had evicted him, the Serrano-Navas family had offered to let Ethan move in with them to finish out the school year. Ethan had used their *teléfono* to call his natural parents to ask permission. "You need to come home to start applying for college," his father had said. "I need you home now," his mother had said.

Ethan had politely declined the Serrano-Navas family's offer, and, with his heart and spirit breaking, he had called his exchange studies adviser and then waited by the phone.

When she had called back to say he'd been booked on a flight leaving in a week and that until then he'd be staying in a hotel, Ethan had whispered the news to Sra. Navas. She had asked him for the phone.

After announcing that he'd be staying with them until the day of his flight, she had hung up the phone and asked Ethan to follow her. In what would have been baby Félix's bedroom, she had told Ethan to consider the room *his* whenever he was in Spain. As she had stood there hugging him with her eyes glistening, Sr. Serrano had carried in Ethan's four suitcases and plopped them down on the bed, a "real" bed with a comfortable mattress. Rebeca and María Luisa had helped Ethan unpack a few things.

Seven days and nights had ticked by—good food, good laughs, good cries, English tutoring, Spanish lessons, dread of going home, fear of a looming divorce. The bed had provoked frustration: *Oh, what could have been.* The ride to the airport that Monday had taken forever, but it hadn't been long enough.

Ethan had been homesick for Spain before the flight attendant announced that the captain had turned off the seatbelt sign. The air over the Atlantic had been turbulent, like Ethan's mood. He had eaten the peanuts and picked at his meal. While changing planes in New York, he had been still far enough from Virginia to feel a mild sense of adventure, but while deplaning in Washington, D.C., his heart and feet had been heavy. His parents had smothered him with their hugs;

he hadn't been so happy to see them. They had stopped for a midnight meal on the long drive home.

The next morning, after sleeping off a bit of jetlag, Ethan had mustered up the courage to drive for the first time in months. He had visited his old Spanish teachers; their accents, which he had once thought were perfect, had sounded flawed to him. After getting a haircut, he had gone on a fruitless search of small-town Bedford for *tomate frito*, and then spent the afternoon in Roanoke checking expiration dates on cans of the fried tomato purée. For dinner he had made green pepper pisto, adding dashes of hot sauce to a smaller batch from the tiny bottle that had become his trademark seemingly after his transition from baby formula to solid food.

His mom had thought the stew would go well over rice; his dad had picked up a loaf of Spanish-style baguette bread on his way home from work. Despite living separately and silently under the same roof, they had been too happy to have Ethan home to infuse the meal with tension. Spanish food, a few laughs, a little crying: Ethan had almost felt like he was back in Las Rozas.

An hour later, when all traces of Spain had been scrubbed off the dishes and wiped off the table, they had set him down to announce their divorce. Ethan had mentally checked in and out of the conversation, paying attention with halfhearted nods or shakes of the head but few words. There was nothing he could have done or said to help them.

And when he wasn't paying attention, his mind had wandered to a place that felt so very far away.

Now, six years later, he was back in Las Rozas. For two weeks, the Serrano-Navas family's *piso* had been his home. The food and the laughs and the cries were still good. Rebeca didn't need him to tutor her in English, but she was still teaching him Spanish. The bed in what would have been baby Félix's room was still "real" and comfortable.

Ethan could walk and talk with his Spanish sisters or shuffle along the sidewalks alone, popping into a bar for a soda pop or to revel in the local dialect and debate during a soccer game on the TV hanging in the corner. He still blushed at commercials with topless women eating spoonfuls of yogurt. At night, when the world outside "his" bedroom was quiet, he still dreaded going home to Virginia, but not because of an impending divorce. His parents had signed that final decree five years ago, and each of them had moved on. But not to better things. A downsizing had forced his father to take a job out of state; an aggressive cancer had reduced his mother to ashes.

21:45 h

The mellow tones of a French horn wandered toward Thomas and Marisa as they sat under a plane tree on the church grounds in Las Rozas. Classical music was usually his white noise, a mask to drown out the stomps and yells and barks of upstairs tenants at the apartment back in the States. But tonight the horn concerto harmonizing the Regiones neighborhood was a welcome distraction from a conversation that had taken an awkward turn toward love and sex.

"Mozart or Haydn," Thomas said, daring to disrupt the silence. "Their music sounds so similar, but . . . I'm guessing it's Mozart."

The radio back home had been on continuously for years, its dust-stuck dial locked on to a classical station. But the announcers distracted him, and he often tuned them out. Classical CDs were voiceless, but closing and stacking the cases took him several minutes. Satellite service offered music channels, but if he switched from cable, an installer would have to invade his "home": drill holes, run and strip cables, displace the TV and power cords. An impossibly messy, lingering, fucking nightmare.

But if the programming package included classical music *and* TV Española Internacional, it might be worth his three hours—likely, a low estimate—of anxious vacuuming, tweaking, checking, rechecking, and re-rechecking after the invasion. The whole Spanish-language package would be a waste of precious dollars, though: damn Mexican shit.

Marisa's antipathy was broader, but she kept it close to the vest, using the pejorative "*sudamericano*—South American," during their conversations to describe anything south of the Rio Grande. And she sneered at criticism from across the pond that the Real Academia Española favored the dialect of Madrid in its signature *Diccionario de la Lengua Española.* "So what?" she had asked Thomas. "Central peninsular Spanish is educated Spanish. Mexicans need to put down their tacos and pick up books."

Few but he had seen the figurative snub of Marisa's Castilian nose.

She did have two friends, gals to catch the latest dubbed flick with or to meet for a lemon beer, but they balked at the kind of conversations she had with Thomas. Struggling with issues of his own, he allowed Marisa to be her wacky, overbearing, arrogant self. And she loved him for it, madly.

Therein lay the problem, and it had lain there quietly for some time. Until tonight.

"I realize Lina's as cute as a damn button," she said, kicking at the blighted leaves on the ground, "but she's not into you. And just because you saw her naked once, years ago, doesn't mean you can't look at another girl. Or is it that you can't look at me?"

Still reeling from Marisa's recent offer to "get down on her knees and kiss him until he felt better," Thomas was caught further off guard. "I look at you, I can look at you. I'm looking at you now."

"You've never looked at *me* the way you look at *her* when no one knows you're looking. Not once."

Thomas inched the zipper farther up his chest and tugged four times at the knot on the bracelet around his wrist. "I thought we had always been honest with each other."

"Not about this."

Her response made him more anxious than angry. Unrequited love was a game of touch-me-not football on a muddy field with uneven goalposts, and Thomas hated to get dirty. But she had been there for him, whisking him away when she saw the episodes coming in order to hide his disorder from the world. And he wanted her in his life; he just didn't *want* her. It would have been so easy if he did.

Marisa's offer echoed in Thomas's head as he tugged again at the knot and forced himself to place his hand on the bench beside hers. "Have I missed some sort of sign along the way?" he asked. "I must have."

Her hand inched closer to his, but she said nothing.

"You know I don't want to leave, but I can't afford to stay: The translations done by machine are cheaper than mine."

"But machine translations are horrible," she said, wrinkling her nose, "and yours are perfect."

"Businesses care more about their bottom line. The work's just not there, so when Óscar asked me to write a column for *El Ágora* and—"

"Óscar's a pompous jerk, by the way," she declared. "I know he just started the company, but he could afford to pay you something. You deserve a little something."

"Until recently, I hadn't given it much thought. Besides, when it comes to writing for Óscar's newspaper, exposure's the real motivation—"

Marisa's thumb brushed Thomas's little finger. "Your speech is much smoother. Is it the music?"

"The music doesn't fix it," he said, glancing at the Plaza Mayor. The orquestra's horns had fallen silent, but its violins were in full voice. *That has to be Mozart.*

It was Beethoven, a concerto.

"I know," she said, "but as you listen to it, that faulty wiring of yours has time to calm down."

"Protein also helps my 'faulty wiring,' as you so politely put it. Those *croquetas* didn't stick with me, and that's half the problem. How about we grab a bite somewhere?"

The famous spaghetti kiss from *La dama y el vagabundo* (*Lady and the Tramp*), flashed into her mind. "Fine by me, and then afterward we can do the other thing."

"What time does the competition start?" he asked.

"At eleven."

"What time is it now?"

"Ten-ish, but I'm not sure." She rarely wore a watch when she was with him. "Do you still want to go if there's time?"

"Only if we're good," he said. "Are we good?"

She ran her toe through the gravel. "You tell me."

Thomas's words came quickly: "We're good, but I'm going to have a hard time forgetting . . ."

"Forgetting what?"

"What you said you'd do for me in that thing over there," he answered, pointing toward the kids' playhouse in the corner of the church grounds. The little building had been vacant since sundown. "And it's going to take a while to ... process the other thing you said, too."

"Do you mean my being in love with you?"

Thomas nodded.

Marisa clasped her hands in her lap. "I've screwed it all up," she sighed. "I thought I could kill two birds, you know. I never imagined you would turn me down."

"You didn't think I was asking you to do that when I told you the release seemed to help?" Thomas asked as he got to his feet.

"No."

"Good," he said, staring at the knot as he reached to help her up. "Because I wasn't."

"I know." She tucked the bracelet inside his sleeve. "At least I can do *that* for you." Delighting in the feel of her hand in his, she slowly stood up. "But you didn't need to ask."

"I never would have," he said. "When you're a freak like me, it's a one-person job."

Marisa's anxiety turned to irritation. The skin on her chest became blotchy. "It doesn't have to be, not in the way you mean. And you're not a freak. I hate it when you say that."

Thomas let go of her hand, but before he could back away she grabbed him by the wrist. "You're not a freak; you have a mental disorder."

"To just about everyone else in the world, there's not much of a difference."

"If we're painting with broad brushes, then the world's full of ignorant jackasses. Screw 'em. We're all touched in the head in one way or another. Hell, I just offered to go down on you in that playhouse. Babies are supposed to *play* in that thing, not be *made* in it."

Thomas couldn't pass up the opportunity to rib her: "You must not know how babies are made if you think what you offered to do—"

"I know how they're made," Marisa declared with a wink and then sat back down. "I also know how they're *not* made." She slipped a hand into her purse and pulled out a condom. She had never used a *profiláctico* before: She had never had a chance or need to. "What if I offered to do something *else* for you?" she asked, desperate to pull

Lina's imaginary hooks out of him.

OCD thrust into Thomas's head an image of children stomping crickets in the playhouse. A moment later he ignored the intrusion and lowered himself back onto the bench. "I thought using birth control was a sin. Aren't you . . . as a Catholic . . . supposed to let God determine the size of your family?"

Marisa was feeling her oats: "I'll be the one to determine that," she said. "And I know what you're doing."

"What am I doing?"

The blotches on Marisa's chest got redder. Her low-cut neckline hadn't drawn any more than the usual attention a man paid to a woman's breasts. "You're turning me down again by changing the subject. Stop changing the subject."

"I don't know what to say," he stuttered, staring at the knot on the bracelet around his wrist. "I'm still trying to process all of this."

Marisa stopped kicking at the blighted leaves and lifted Thomas's chin with her hand. "There are worse things than a woman telling you she loves you and then offering to make you feel better."

Thomas struggled for a response but finally found one: "Give me some time. I need time."

She gently shook Thomas by the chin. "You'd be lucky to have me, you know."

"I know."

They sat quietly until Thomas broke the silence: "We need to get going, but may I say something without getting into trouble?"

"That depends on what you're going to say."

Thomas spoke anyway: "I don't want to have to, well, keep fighting off your advances. Do you have a way to . . . calm your frustration?"

Marisa chuckled. "I love you, but I'm not sexually frustrated: I've got a toy to help with that."

Thomas couldn't help smiling as he gestured toward the church. "Maybe you should pop in for a quick confession. Three Hail Marys, an Our Father or two, and you'd be good to go."

She chuckled again. "Maybe you should join me, you hairy-palmed sinner."

"Only if you promise to use the kneeler in the way God intended."

23:25 h

The *plaza de toros* was half empty, but the poor attendance was by no means an indictment against the sport of bullfighting. The older generations were at home, doing the dishes or snoozing in front of dubbed American reruns; the younger generation was at the fiestas, riding the rides, drinking, and flirting. And the action in the ring wasn't a classic bullfight, with matadors wearing sparkling suits of lights and bulls falling for the deceit of their capes; it was a *concurso de recortadores*.

The competition pitted duos of acrobatic bullfighters (men *and* women) in tennis shoes and sweats against a two- to three-year-old bull. Each team had ten minutes to place as many doughnut-sized rings on the bull's horns as possible. Currently, the lead was three, and if the fireball hadn't put the fear of God in one of the men as time expired, it would have been four.

Although Churro's only role as a secondary had been to lure the bull away from the downed competitor, his pulse still raced. Vigilant, he grabbed two fistfuls of the capote at his feet, kicked open the magenta-and-yellow canvas, and bit down on its collar as he straightened. Holding the cape with his teeth, he folded his arms around it and then slipped again behind burladero number three, the wooden shield closest to the young bull's *querencia*, the spot to which he tended to return.

Except for the creature's wonky horn, in coloration, size, and temperament he was a dead ringer for the second bull Churro had fought earlier that day. The double take that he had done when the animal trotted out of the *toril* gate was just a knee jerk of wishful thinking. That bull was dead, a casualty of ten minutes of artless butchery Churro could never get back. Mercedes had wept as the mule team dragged the corpse out of the ring.

The creature with the wonky horn now scrabbling the sand of its querencia would die outside the ring, quickly, shot between the eyes in the shed that served as a slaughterhouse.

"Thank God," Churro mumbled into his capote.

SATURDAY, 5 OCTOBER 2002

Las Rozas, Spain

02:30 h

Headlights filtered through the tree outside Avenida de la Constitución, 16, dappling Ethan's sweater as he stared out the window at the Iglesia de San Miguel. Except for a pair of sconces flanking the rear nave doors, the church named after the town's patron saint was dark.

In the corner of the courtyard, near a grouping of beech saplings planted by the hand of God, he could make out a picnic table. It was now scratched with names, but the once smooth top had been a handy place to do English classwork whenever María Luisa's intrusions drove Ethan and his tutee from the apartment.

Rebeca had no real need for the language after finishing the school year that he had not. Although his tutelage bore short-lived fruit, a reality that peeved him from time to time, he had fond memories of mispronunciations such as vanilla "snakes" and french fries with "kapchüp." And despite his cock of a host father's verbal booting, Ethan's reminiscences of those six months brought a smile to his rounding face.

During his exchange stay, life had been as simple as his kiddie days. He had served the four-year sentence of high school, earned his 4.0, and deferred applying to college, at which he would have likely dredged for four years at his parents' insistence. He had never shown an iota of interest in going. In the interim, he had been the blackboard on which invaluable experience was chalked, from the first *"buenos días"* in the morning to the last *"hasta mañana"* at night.

He still resented his parents' declining the Serrano-Navas family's offer, and he could not forgive his host parents for provoking the decision in the first place. But he hadn't been blameless in the matter.

"You become *imposible*," his host mother used to scold him after calls from his natural mother. Those conversations about her marital discord had taken their toll on him. But he had been only a teenager and poorly equipped to handle the disintegration of a marriage.

During his short walks alone—it was the "alone" that had made his host mother bristle—to the BurgoCentro to buy his favorite lime-and-cola candies, he had tried to decipher his emotions, picturing the distant *"How Are You Feeling Today?"* poster hanging in his room. Identifying *how* he was feeling had always been difficult for him, so his occasional therapist had prescribed the art print. It depicted thirty faces showing different emotions; "impossible" wasn't one of them.

CONFUSED, SAD, DEPRESSED, LONELY, and ANXIOUS were the faces that had best described his mother. She had burdened her son with those emotions. Her burdening him had made Ethan ANGRY, FRUSTRATED, DISGUSTED, and ENRAGED; his allowing her to do so had made him hate himself, and he had been taught never to hate anyone.

When Ethan managed to stand up for himself and say no, he felt guilty or anxious. He avoided debates, along with conflict and mirrors. Not that he had done things for which he couldn't look himself in the eye. No, he just thought he was ugly.

The receding hairline took his average looks with it. The braces-straightened teeth, dingy from the iron tonic he had taken as a child, gnawed at his self-image. The bowed legs bent the way he saw himself. But he had discovered a way to straighten the view, slightly. By tying a sock below each knee and turning the knots inward, he could force the inseams of his pants outward. The lumps needed occasional adjustments, but his khakis hung straight—a trick of cotton underpinning the illusion of self-esteem.

But Ethan did hold one trump, a card he could play almost innately to take whatever hand school, family, or genetics had dealt him. Álvaro insisted that the Church had struck reincarnation from the Bible out of self-interest, and maybe he was right: Ethan's tongue could have been Spanish in a previous life.

When it came to the language, he was a crack. No high school junior in central Virginia had been his equal, one of sixty chosen statewide to attend the month-long Governor's Spanish Academy. After taking an oath to speak only Spanish—except for honest mistakes, violating the *juramento* had led to immediate expulsion—

the students had been unknowingly grouped according to their ability. Ethan had been one of the ten "most gifted," and he had vied for the top spot with a whiz from northern Virginia. The friendly competition had made each of them better. Ethan had cried when he was released from his oath.

Senior year of high school, he had been generous with what he had learned at the Academy, but he had still displayed his skills modestly, with only the barest hint of the trepidation that plagued him outside the world of *ñ*'s and *rr*'s. After cakewalking to the Spanish Award, he had turned his gold tassel with a smile, which continued to broaden throughout the hot Virginia summer. When his exchange experience had begun in late September, his passion for Spain was burning.

His mood had cooled a bit in December, when his host parents became as chilly as the weather. On *Nochevieja*, New Year's Eve (and literally "old night"), being invisible to the opposite sex had gotten as "old" as the "night." But when the Serrano-Navas family had begun to take him under its wing, he found his smile again, only to have it completely wiped off his face when his host father had evicted him three months later.

Afterward, Ethan had kept himself sharp by reading the newspapers he had bought while waiting for his flight and then crammed into his carry-ons. He had preserved his impeccable pronunciation using a microcassette recorder.

As he stared out the window at the church named after Las Rozas's patron saint, that same recorder now lay on the windowsill in front of him. But the voice on the microcassette was his mother's.

Diagnosed with a glioblastoma in late May, she had quickly fallen victim to the aggressive brain tumor and died on the fourth of August while Ethan was at work. He had spread her ashes on the Blue Ridge Parkway, at Porter's Mountain Overlook, on one of those rare summer evenings he could see the Peaks of Otter from his apartment. Wanting a tangible place to pay his respects, he had buried a few ashy bone fragments at the base of a pear-shaped boulder.

He had gone back to her "grave" twice, but he hadn't listened to her taped message to him even once. Returning to the site for a third time without having heard her message would be disrespectful and cowardly, even in his timid estimation. He had brought the tape with him to Spain.

On Monday morning, Ethan insisted, watching an off-duty taxi roll down Avenida de la Constitución. *María Luisa can press* PLAY *if I can't.* He had promised his aunt to listen to the tape while he was in Spain, and to that promise, like those he made to everyone else, he would be faithful. The promises he made to himself were much harder to keep.

07:43 h

Las Rozas was stirring to life. A bottled gas delivery truck clanged past the open window, but Thomas was already awake. Staring at the clock he had watched throughout the night, he sat hunched on the side of the bed, his forearm resting on the nightstand. He dared not move the travel alarm, so he pinched it lightly between his index finger and thumbnail, which quivered over a small button split into half-moons marked ALARM and SET.

07:45 h

Thomas took a shallow breath, held it, and pressed the button before the alarm could ring for the fifth time. Five would have been bad: It wasn't one of his numbers. After letting the echo fade, he pressed the button again and then stared at the display, holding his breath again. *It's there.*

"It" was a little bell above the colon that indicated the alarm was turned on. A lingering touch—he had a proclivity for lingering touches—could have turned it off altogether, but his nail had been quick. He exhaled. The alarm was ready for tomorrow morning, and it was important that it was . . . irrationally important, anxiety-provokingly important. He lifted his elbow off the nightstand and sat back. *It's done.*

But no amount of physical distance could have taken his mind off that bell or prevented his daily battle with "it," as even a master of self-control is helpless against spasmodic contractions of the diaphragm. He leaned forward. *It's there.*

It was there. He clearly saw it and the speck of dust on it, but he couldn't take his eyes off it. He tried to lean back. *It's done. It's there. It isn't.* He sighed and checked it again. The thoughts became reflexes.

I see it. It's right there. He leaned back, but before his spine could straighten, he threw himself forward. *Damn. Last time,* he emptily promised with all his heart and rechecked it.

In the distance a driver laid on the horn, but Thomas was already beyond the tipping point again. *Not there. Damn it, shit, hell. Last time, I promise.* He re-rechecked it, but was soon lost in the bell once again.

It's there. No, I see it. Fight it. It's not, check it later. . . I might forget. Last time, I promise. He re-rechecked it again, raised his eyes to heaven, and then smacked himself on the head. At that moment, he wasn't sure whom he hated more. *Guaranteed done, no matter what. I promise.*

There was no way in hell he was done.

You're not getting anything else from me. I promise just one last time. He checked it, but he wasn't really seeing it anymore. Something similar to the difference between hearing and listening.

07:47 h

It's there, it's there, it's there, it's there, Thomas insisted, desperate for the relief that often came with repetition in fours. He could have afforded to change the plane ticket if he had one euro (about a dollar and thirty cents) for each time he'd repeated something four times in September alone.

Four was one of his lucky numbers. His other ones included seventeen, twenty-seven, thirty-seven, and forty-four, but when he used those, things took quite a while longer, and he had to get going. No, four usually did the trick. Besides, the higher numbers were better suited for turning off headlights, wiping down the bathtub, blowing dust off the television, walking across a room, and closing bottles. He could have stayed in Las Rozas forever if he had one euro for each time he had mashed the refrigerator handle.

He took several deep breaths, trying to reset the brain that wasn't getting the message.

Whether the cause of his OCD was abnormal biology, psychology, or, more likely, a combination of the two, he took no pleasure in his obsessions and compulsions. He was suffering.

07:48 h

Thomas wiped the "pollution" of sweat and natural oil off his finger and wagged the tip of it across the display, playing peekaboo with the bell. *There, not there. There, not there.*

Muttering stares were often just fists to the chest, but taps and rubs could be like paddles to a fibrillating heart and restore normal rhythm to his brain; for Thomas, abnormal was normal. The additional stimuli helped curb his anxiety, so he relied heavily on the sense of touch during his private struggles, but in public the behaviors drew embarrassing looks, so he disguised them.

When tapping and rubbing didn't provide the necessary relief, the situation worsened still, and he was often forced into momentary, even persistent surrender. But if he was playing beat the clock or if the task was especially difficult, he resorted to more severe behaviors to increase the stimulus. Metal zipper pulls were tugged so hard they bent. Plastic caps were tightened until they bulged at the sides; often they were so tight he had to open them with pliers. The violent rattling of the side door used to shake and wake the house.

Thomas was incredibly sorry about breaking the doorknob.

07:49 h

It's there.

The next few moments were critical, so Thomas sat breathless, motionless, fearing the unexpected, even the rumble of his stomach.

07:50 h

On to the bracelet, the shirt tag, the drawstring in the pajama pants, in that order. In that order.

The day had just begun.

He was exhausted.

08:50 h

Pamplona had honored its patron saint, San Fermín, with nightly bacchanalia that stretched into morning and with renowned *encierros*, runnings of the bulls. Las Rozas's *Fiestas de San Miguel* were merry yet fairly sober and inexpensive festivities; the encierros were the subject of only local chatter. And though the bulls were smaller and slower than those run during the *Sanfermines*, their horns were no less indifferent to human suffering.

Following its usual route through Las Rozas, the local brass band had tooted and drummed the town awake. Roceños of all ages and sizes and shapes were gathered for another encierro. A five hundred-meter (one thousand six hundred forty–foot) block party: red wine in *bota* bags, *sardinas* and chorizo over charcoal, loaves of baguette bread, horn players, boisterous spectators, confident winks, anxious smiles, tightly laced running shoes, ubiquitous red scarves.

The course was built daily by men wearing blue coveralls. Sturdy posts wedged into permanent holes, crossbeams lashed or clamped in place, scaffolds, street trees boarded up with makeshift ladders, shuttered storefronts. And when the encierro was over, all of it was torn down.

The course varied slightly from year to year, diverted by improvements to the growing town, but the traditional start was on Avenida Constitución, outside La Rinconera. This year's fiestas were no exception: a boon for business that had Sr. Serrano opening early.

The short stretch between the livestock delivery truck and the Plaza Mayor was dangerous; the corner itself was deadly. After bursting out of the truck, the bulls were instantly on the cocky and dewy-eyed teenagers thronging in front of the plaza and on its steps. Without a fence across the small square, the spectators were also fair game.

At the Plaza Mayor, the course turned left onto the long Avenida Toreros, along which the wiser runners waited. The *avenida* ran through the Regiones neighborhood, doglegging between the fountain of the Virgen de la Retamosa and the Plaza de España, and then ended into a narrow street. A left turn, a short stretch, a traffic circle, an access road that stretched past a vacant lot, the temporary plaza de toros.

All that was needed this morning were the bulls, but an accident had the truck stuck in traffic.

María Luisa, Rebeca, Álvaro, and Ethan chatted near the fountain. The girls had been chatting up friends there since earning their independence from Mamá and Papá. During last year's fiestas, Rebeca had gotten soaked while watching a humorous gymkhana— *note to self: don't wear white along obstacle courses*, she had thought, blushing, her nipples hard under a thin bra. But the fountain was now dry thanks to a godforsaken pump and the local drought; the statue of the virgin had become a roost for pigeons, and they had defiled her.

"So gross," Rebeca said. "Álvaro, is that stuff damaging the concrete?"

"Pigeon droppings are acidic, so yes."

Rebeca frowned. "I wish I had a hose or a bucket."

"As if you'd do any manual labor," María Luisa sneered.

"You're one to talk," Rebeca said, annoyed: a longstanding annoyance between mismatched siblings. "When's the last time you—" She was interrupted by a man sporting a bright red shirt.

"At least twenty more minutes," the member of the bullfighting club said. He handed Álvaro a sandwich wrapped in tinfoil and then offered one to Ethan and the girls, who each politely refused.

"*No jodas*—Holy shit," Álvaro said flatly.

"The breeder's going to get an earful." The man hurried along.

"I'd rather not stand here for twenty more minutes," Rebeca said, looking around. Her eyes settled on the Plaza de España. "Does anyone want to go window-shopping with me?"

Álvaro's mind was wandering to the now delayed run ahead: "I'm good," he said vaguely.

María Luisa rolled her eyes at her sister. *What's there to look at? One shop.*

"Ethan?" Rebeca asked.

Ethan continued to stare at his pant legs, which were slightly bowed without the knotted socks to make them hang straight: *They would have fallen off during the run and tripped me up.*

"Ethan," Rebeca said with a poke, rousing him.

He tore his eyes off the abomination. "Don't you want to go?" he asked Álvaro, who answered with a polite shake of the head. "I'm game, then."

"You're wasting his time," María Luisa told her sister. "Ethan, let me take you into Madrid when the good shops are actually open."

"Maybe later," Rebeca cheeped, snatching Ethan by the cuff, "but now he's coming with me." The pair squeezed through the barrier.

"Surprise, surprise," María Luisa grumbled, watching them go.

Álvaro was mindlessly eating his sandwich. Yesterday, he and the other runners had gotten cooked ham, but this morning it was Spain's ubiquitous air-cured ham. Álvaro didn't care much for *jamón serrano*, but he was crazy about Rebeca. Frustrated by the delay, he took an angry bite. *Twenty minutes*, he scoffed inwardly before slowly beginning to feel foolish. He took another bite, a softer one. *Ten minutes . . . twenty minutes is nothing in a lifetime together. Nothing*, he repeated, *but I do want to prove myself.*

More mindless chewing, but as he finished the sandwich, his thoughts became focused. An old bullfighting magazine and an interview with Juan Belmonte, perhaps Spain's greatest matador: *The way you fight reveals who you are*, Álvaro quoted him. He paced for a moment and then tweaked the legend's words to match the situation: *The way you run reveals who you are.*

María Luisa eyed the window-shoppers as they lingered at the antique shop. *She's doing it just to piss me off.* After a huff, she shook off the unpleasantness and turned to her future brother-in-law. It was a good time to follow up on a prior bit of meddling. "Have there been any new developments?"

"No," Álvaro muttered before balling up the tinfoil.

"Did you at least talk to her?"

"Twice."

"Twice? Wow, good for you."

Between the cigarette butts and empty *pipas*, sunflower seeds (Spaniards ate them by the millions), there was enough litter in the thirsty fountain. Álvaro stuck the foil ball in his pocket. "We talked last night and again this morning."

"And Rebeca still wants to wait until you're married?"

"She's emphatic."

María Luisa frowned. "June's a long time away." She did the math: "eight months."

"I know," Álvaro sighed, "but she's worth waiting for."

"Probably, but it's still got to be frustrating. I hope you're getting *some* sort of satisfaction."

"Above the waist: your father's cardinal rule."

María Luisa frowned again. "He will disown her if there are three of you at the altar," she said, simulating a pregnant belly.

"I have absolutely no doubt about that."

"He values you as a waiter, but thinks of you as a son."

Álvaro rocked in place.

"But he's already lost one son, may Félix rest in peace. He doesn't want to have to handle the loss of another."

"They would never find my body."

"Not in one piece," María Luisa said, "but that's not what I meant." She inched forward. "He'd fire you, for starters, yes—"

"In a heartbeat."

"But he wants her out," she continued with a check over her shoulder. "He wants both of us out, and if you get so frustrated that you call it off, no one wins. No one." A wry smile, a touch on the arm. "And Father's no hypocrite."

"*¿Hipócrita?*"

"Do as I say, not as I do."

Looking skyward, Álvaro took a deep breath. "What exactly are you saying?" he seemed to ask the heavens.

"I'm saying," María Luisa explained, "that somewhere behind Papá's scowl there's a part of him that remembers what it's like to be a young man in love. And I'm saying that just because Rebeca's still a virgin— You know she didn't give it up to Hermán, right?"

"That's what she assured me," Álvaro said.

"She didn't; we were much closer then. Anyway, just because she wants to remain a virgin in the traditional sense, doesn't mean she can't lend you a hand at the very least."

"Did she—"

"Hermán got nothing," María Luisa repeated. "She's not seventeen any more, though, and even good girls have urges. Push carefully, but push. If you're lucky, maybe she'll—"

"We're done," Álvaro interrupted. Even if he hadn't caught sight of Rebeca and Ethan heading back, the conversation was over.

09:45 h

The bulls had been run and penned: bumps, bruises, scratches— nothing serious. The men in blue coveralls were stacking posts, crossbeams, and scaffolding on curbsides and in trucks. The ring of sledgehammers punctuated sidewalk conversations. The length of the course was open to traffic, but everyday encounters with cars, *motos*, and scooters seemed like an alien invasion.

Except for their dusty clothing, Ethan and Álvaro were no worse for the wear as they began the walk up Avenida Toreros. As usual, the girls had not run and were waiting.

"When I was an exchange student," Ethan said, "the bullring was just past the farmers market."

"I remember. I think I liked it there better."

"When did they move it?"

"A while ago. It's all the way down here," Álvaro said, anticipating the next question, "because by making the course longer, they've spread the runners out a bit. Too many kids were getting hurt in the logjam at the start."

"Including Rebeca."

Álvaro could still see her lying there: bloody knee, panicked look on her face. "She was nearly trampled before I could pick her up."

"And she hasn't run since."

Álvaro smiled. "Not even once."

"María Luisa's never run," Ethan said, trying to imagine her hoofing it down the course. "She likes to watch, though."

"María Luisa likes to do a lot of things."

"Such as?"

Álvaro put his arm around him. They weren't brothers, but it felt like it. "Apparently, she's an expert on sex and dating, too."

"That's news to me."

"She thinks the next time I go to undo Rebeca's bra, I should try her pants instead."

"Really?" Ethan asked, not completely surprised.

"Yeah, she's afraid I'm going to get frustrated and call it off."

"The engagement?"

"Yeah, and if I do, 'no one wins. No one.' I'm supposed to 'push carefully, but push.'"

Bells went off in Ethan's head: "She has an agenda."

"Bingo, señor, but what is it?"

Ethan didn't usually think well on his feet, but more than one idea popped into his head. "Rebeca's bedroom is larger and has two windows. María Luisa's 'dungeon,' as Rebeca calls it, *is* pretty dark. Maybe she wants to move into it after the wedding."

"I thought of that," Álvaro said, "but that seems more like a sad opportunity than a motive, especially for a grown woman who needs to move out instead of across the hall."

"Money's tight right now."

"Well, she better get her act together because Sr. Serrano wants both of his daughters out, and—"

Ethan's brow furrowed. "Where did you—"

"María Luisa told me. I can't imagine he won't lay down the law once his younger daughter's out of the house."

"I think you're right," Ethan agreed. "The relationship María Luisa has with her father is regrettable."

"It's crippling, emotionally and physically," Álvaro said almost sadly. "Except for an occasional girls' night out, she lives like a nun, a nun with doughnuts."

"She eats to fill the hole in her heart."

"Just how big *is* that hole?"

"Big," Ethan said, "and there are probably two of them, although the second one seems smaller."

"Two?"

"Sra. Navas doesn't seem to understand her or to even like her at times."

"I've noticed that, too," Álvaro said. "It's a sad situation, but my future sister-in-law needs to mind her own business. And that know-it-all attitude of hers . . . *¡Joder!*"

"I don't hear it as much as you do," Ethan fibbed; "there's just a hint of it in her letters."

"It's pervasive," Álvaro declared.

"I'm no expert, but I think she's trying to feel important and to be heard."

"You're making excuses for her?"

"I'm just saying that . . . maybe it's low self-esteem."

Álvaro put his arm around him again. "We all have our moments and our problems. How we handle them is what matters."

"*Amén*," Ethan said.

Álvaro stared up the avenida, debating whether to have their first, real conversation about the death of Ethan's mother. It wasn't the time. "My—"

"I am curious—"

"Go ahead," Álvaro said.

"Sorry. I am curious, though, about your getting 'frustrated.' Tell me to shut up, but—"

"Ask whatever you want."

"Well, I wasn't sure. So . . . are you?"

Álvaro didn't hesitate: "Very. Especially when she lets me play with the button on that pair of jeans with the hearts on the back pockets. Damn, she looks good in those jeans, and she knows it."

"And?"

"Then she smacks my hand if my fingers head any farther south, and I go to the bathroom for some alone time."

"And then to confession," Ethan joked.

"Confession?"

Ethan lowered his voice: "You're Catholic; everything's a sin."

"Not whacking off."

"I don't follow."

"When I was young," Álvaro explained, "Grandma had a parakeet named Zafi. He was royal blue with a pale purple beak, just the most beautiful bird I had ever seen, and very sweet; Grandma said God was smiling when he made Zafi. But for the longest time I wondered why God would have made a creature that, well, pleasured himself on his perch."

"Really?"

Álvaro laughed. "Make no mistake about it, Zafi humped that stick, and that behavior I had been told repeatedly was a sin. So one day I stopped pretending not to see it and asked Grandma if I, too, was one of God's creatures. She said that I was, so then I asked why she chuckled when he did it, but I had to talk to a priest after she caught me doing it."

"And what was her answer?" Ethan asked.

"Something like 'God gave us mastery over the creatures of the earth, and since we're God's creatures, we're supposed to be masters of ourselves, too, and abstain from behaviors we know are wrong.'"

"Huh?"

"That was my reaction, too," Álvaro said. "So then I asked how we know *that* behavior is wrong. 'The Bible tells us so,' she said."

"Something about someone spilling his seed on the ground," Ethan said.

"It's the ultimate 'because I said so.'"

"I hate that answer."

"It's a dodge," Álvaro agreed. "I'll never use it with my kids."

"But you said your grandmother chuckled when Zafi did it."

"Nervous laughter."

"I can see that," Ethan said. "My dad's deodorant failed him when we had 'the talk.'"

"I think Grandma was more nervous about her faith."

"Her faith?"

Álvaro waved to the girls, who had begun to walk toward them. "I think she's too smart to be truly devout. Most of us are too smart to be truly devout. Like most of us, Grandma's afraid, afraid of her own mortality, to be precise."

"That there's nothing after this," Ethan said.

"*Exacto.* So she submits herself to religion, believing in truths that are supposedly beyond her understanding."

"I'm with you."

"But those truths are just ideas that are accepted as true. When Grandma was a little girl, did she really have a choice not to accept them?"

"Not really, especially in fascist Spain," Ethan said.

"There's no such thing as a Catholic child, a Jewish child, or a Muslim child, just a child of Catholic parents and so on. By the time Grandma was old enough to think for herself, she had been subjected to so much persuasion that her newfound doubts made her anxious."

"I know exactly what you're saying."

"Grandma is so afraid that little voice is wrong," Álvaro conjectured, "that she's compelled to believe."

"Noah gathered the animals two by two, and Jonah hung out in a great fish?"

"A sane person knows deep down those things never happened; take his or her protestations with a grain of salt. Most of those tales are metaphors or parables, but whatever they are doesn't matter. There's a tremendous sense of calm that accompanies belief, so Grandma blissfully turns a blind eye to whatever doesn't fit."

"But isn't that being dishonest?" Ethan asked.

"I wouldn't call it dishonest."

"Well, then, what would you call it?"

"Chemistry."

"Chemistry?"

"*¡Hola, guapa!*—Hello, gorgeous!" Álvaro yelled to Rebeca before lowering his voice. "Zafi rubbed his perch because it felt good; Grandma believes because it makes her feel good."

"Then why did she laugh?"

"Because, when you're looking at a bird as beautiful as Zafi, it's hard to pretend you're blind."

11:00 h

Mercedes pushed the silverware drawer tight against the face frame and then pushed it again. She rummaged through the drawer below. "That's the only one I have," she told Marisa, neatening the clutter before easing the drawer closed and giving it the same treatment. "Can you squeeze any out of it at all?"

"Not a drop, but thanks for looking."

"And you're sure you don't have something that might work? Clear nail polish?"

"I don't wear clear," Marisa said; "for me, it's yellow and only yellow." She sighed. "Besides, superglue worked before, so that's what I need. He won't trust anything else."

"Shame the hardware store was out. Did you try the one hundred pesetas store?"

"They only had white glue. And they changed the name when we converted to the euro, remember?"

"I know they don't call it that anymore. Force of habit for an old gal like me."

Perturbed, Marisa banged the useless tube against the table.

"Beating it to death won't do any good, sweetie," Mercedes said, moving toward the stove. "You're at a dead end, I take it."

"I'll check the BurgoCentro—"

"I'm not talking about glue." She lit one of the burners with a cigarette lighter. "Feel like a lime blossom tea? I'm going to have one."

"Mucho."

Mercedes filled her favorite saucepan and placed it back on the burner. After nudging the pan's handle parallel with the front controls, she took two teabags out of a small tin that once held a sewing kit (the other wedding gift from her mother). "Don't lose hope," she said and sat down at the table.

"All I have is hope. Well, that's not exactly true. I probably still have a red face from last night. How does my face look?"

"Beautiful, as usual," Mercedes said, smiling. "I'm sure you just caught him by surprise."

"To say the least."

"Does he—"

"But now that I think about it," Marisa said, *"how* could he not have seen it?"

"Maybe he didn't know the depth of your feelings . . . had just a hint."

"Well, he certainly knows I'm crazy about him now."

"Not many men would have turned down your, well, bold offer. I admire his values, always have."

Marisa picked at the tablecloth. "They're part of what I love about him, but . . ."

"But what?"

"But apparently, none of him loves *me*."

"He loves you," Mercedes said without hesitation; "he just isn't *in love* with you right now. But that could change."

"I don't see how. He's crazy about *her*."

"But *she's* not crazy about *him*, far from it." Mercedes craned her neck to see into the saucepan. Tiny bubbles were forming.

"It kills me," Marisa humphed.

"What kills you, sweetie?"

"Cascalina. Lina and I used to be good friends. Now I can't stand to look at that skinny, little witch."

"It's a pity you girls were delayed that morning," Mercedes said, getting to her feet. "And unfortunate for you that he walked in on her by accident."

"I'm not sure that's when it started, but it surely was the end for my chances."

From the drying rack beside the sink, Mercedes took two spotless cups and saucers, which she placed on the table, and turned off the burner. She neatly opened the teabags, placed one in each cup, and slowly poured the water.

"Thanks."

She returned the pan to the stove and handed Marisa two teaspoons. "How about a little something to eat?"

Marisa nodded.

Mercedes carefully reached into the basket on top of the refrigerator, took out two packages of fairy cakes, and placed one beside each cup of tea. A cooled jar of orange marmalade and an opener were already on the table.

While the tea steeped, Marisa stewed.

11:30 h

The gazebo in the center of the Plaza de España still smelled of paint, but, similar to the rest of the *Meseta* (Spain's vast, central plateau), it was bone dry. The wood had been scraped and sanded in preparation for painting, but the finished coat was far from smooth.

"That's just like city hall," Álvaro said, sliding his hand across the railing behind Rebeca.

"City hall? What are you talking about?"

"Cheap paint."

Rebeca gathered her hair into a ponytail as she leaned forward. "How can you tell it's cheap?"

"The better paints self-level," Álvaro said with a hint of masculine puff. "When this stuff peels off, *they'll* have to paint it again, and *we'll* have to pay for it."

"'Never skimp on paint, toilet paper, or mattresses,' Papá says."

Álvaro agreed. "And that reminds me, what did you find out about that piso in Majadahonda?"

"The apartment's currently under contract, but the realtor thinks another one in the same building will become available after the holidays. I know how much you like that location, so I told her you'd be in touch."

"Didn't you mean 'we like'?" Álvaro asked hopefully.

"No, I meant 'you,' and we've already had this conversation. Yes, Majadahonda's less expensive than Las Rozas, and still close, very close. But that piso is across the street from a Pryca; I told you I don't want to look at a parking lot full of grocery carts."

"Well, did she tell you on which side of the building the other one is located?"

"It's on the back."

"You'd have a view of the courtyard instead. Even better."

Rebeca shifted in her seat and became oddly quiet.

"Or is there some other problem?"

She rewrapped her ponytail.

"Come on, out with it," Álvaro pressed.

"Majadahonda's only a good walk from here."

"And?"

"It's too close. I need more of a buffer."

"From what? From whom?"

Rebeca hesitated to answer, a curious change for someone who seemed to love the sound of her own voice. She began to stare at the rooftops of the Regiones neighborhood. The bell tower of the Iglesia de San Miguel jutted into the sky like a stony middle finger. She had lived in its shadow her entire life, but her true feelings were about to see the light of day.

"Rebeca?"

"I'd like to move far from here."

Stunned, Álvaro sat back. "Where's this coming from?" he managed to ask.

Rebeca said nothing as her eyes trailed down the bell tower until it disappeared behind rooftop condensers. Her gaze moved lower still, the visual journey now one of memory: the subtle change in color where new stones were laid on old ones after La Guerra, the red nave doors with black strap hinges, the granite benches.

She spent countless hours in reverie leaning on the railing of her family's balcony, and, except for seasonal pots of thyme and peppermint, she was alone—no disapproving father, no pious mother, no meddling sister. Upstairs, Álvaro's grandmother stepped outside only long enough to water her carnations, calling down to Rebeca to warn her. Downstairs, patrons of her father's taberna came and went with confirming bobs of the head or the occasional greeting, to which she responded warmly but without excess.

Although her reputation as a chatterbox was well deserved, she actually preferred quiet. But not all silence in the Serrano-Navas family's home was golden, especially around the dinner table. There, her father's chair was more like a soapbox, so Rebeca filled the silence to steer the conversation in safe directions: the good works of Franco, the bulls, and *fútbol*, soccer.

Like many working-class Madrileños, Sr. Serrano had been an Atlético Madrid man his entire life. He took his loyalty to "*Los Colchoneros*—the Mattressmakers" so far as to refuse to set foot in the stadium of their city rival in white, Real Madrid, the New York Yankees of world football.

With high hopes for a footballer in the family, he had put Félix in a red-and-white-striped diaper shirt for the trip home from the hospital, but that dream died with his boy. María Luisa had stopped playing in a girls' league soon after and became an armchair striker. Rebeca didn't care much for fútbol. She did enjoy changing the subject to recent games and watching her father and her know-it-all sister kick each other in the figurative shins.

Álvaro rested his palm on Rebeca's knee. "It's your sister, isn't it?"

"What makes you think María Luisa has anything to do with this?"

"She's been a busy not-so-little bee."

"What do you mean?" Rebeca asked anxiously.

"She gave me relationship advice while you and Ethan were window-shopping."

"Álvaro, so help me God, if you talked to her about your wandering fingers."

It was his turn to squirm. "She's afraid I can't wait until our wedding night, but I certainly can—"

"Did you tell her about your coping mechanism?"

"I had to reassure her," he said. Pulling a Rebeca, he then changed the subject: "Ethan attributes her proclivity for giving advice to low self-esteem."

"Ethan? Is that what you two were talking about?" she gasped. "Why don't you tell Papá, too? I'm sure he'd love to hear about my 'virtue.' And don't forget about Mamá. She could add you to her prayer list."

It was no secret that Rebeca was saving herself for the honeymoon, and though the sarcasm was understandable, Álvaro sensed self-rebuke in her words. "Why are you mocking your virtue?"

After an uneasy silence, Álvaro's Rebeca came back to him. "Ignore what I said. I was just angry."

"That's okay."

"I'm not good at being angry. Sorry."

"And I'm sorry for not walking away when she started talking. But just because María Luisa is the person who uttered the words, doesn't mean they weren't worth hearing."

"What words?"

Álvaro glanced around. Except for a few pigeons and a ragged-clothed twosome searching the tables of Café Sol, the plaza slumbered. "She said you have urges, and judging by your response, I think she was right. How could she not be right? And if she was wrong, our relationship is in trouble."

"Álvaro, dear, of course I have urges, but nothing good ever comes from a lapse in judgment. Besides, Papá would kill me if a 'seaman' ever slipped past the harbor patrol.' And we'd never see Mamá again. She spends enough time alone in her bedroom praying already."

In the spirit of candor, Álvaro pushed his luck, quietly. "That 'seaman' wouldn't be naked, you know. He'd be wearing a rubber raincoat, maybe one with ribs that would feel really good."

"Álvaro Perona!"

He continued to push. "Rebeca, I want to spend the rest of my life with you, whether you make me wait to have sex or not. Somewhere in that beautiful head of yours, above those perfect, tasty breasts, you know that. You *know* that." He pushed harder. "But I'm not some pervert for wanting to touch you and to be touched by you. For you to repeatedly deny me anything but self-release must be a power trip, a lack of desire for me, or a convenient mix of the two."

Álvaro immediately regretted the outburst.

"I need to go," Rebeca said.

"Now?"

"I'm not mad. I just need to talk to someone."

"Who?"

She pointed toward the church. "Come for lunch. Mamá is making lentils. Don't be late."

"Rebeca, I—" He grabbed her hand, interlacing their fingers.

"I'm sorry I make you feel that way."

Álvaro's thumb caressed her palm.

"I'm not mad. I just need to talk to someone," she repeated, pointing again toward the church. "You have to let me go, or nothing's going to get any better."

Álvaro kissed her on the back of the hand and reluctantly released her fingers.

She bent and kissed him on the cheek. "See you at lunch. Don't be late," she said and then left.

Álvaro stared at her ass as she marched away. "God was smiling when he made her, too."

12:15 h

A tall, dark-skinned rag tossed himself onto a bench near Café Sol. The concrete slapped his emaciated butt—a light sentence for the petty thief. "That guy has left," he said with a thick Andalusian accent. "You coming?"

His much shorter partner responded in the affirmative and grabbed a cosmetic case with a duct-taped handle.

Their vulturous eyes searched the cobblestones as they walked toward the gazebo. Still nothing but pigeon droppings. Once inside, they scavenged for coins and then placed three dowels of bracelets between them and set about making more. The cool shade was welcome relief, near the shoppers yet far enough from the shops to keep them out of trouble with the *Guardia Civil*, the beatings still fresh in their minds and on their backs.

Pickings during the just-ended fiestas in Majadahonda had been slim anyway—a torn leather cushion and two rusty razor blades from the bottom of a Dumpster. They had migrated to Las Rozas, where they had been slinking around since Wednesday.

The younger generation's demand for their type of leatherwork was high, but so was the supply this time of year. To broaden their offerings and stave off hunger, the tag team had recently filched bootleg CDs in Madrid. They kept their ill-gotten wares under a blanket in the bottom of the cosmetic case and displayed them sporadically. When even their expanded "product line" left them wanting, targeted intimidation proved an effective sales technique. And they weren't above snatching purses or picking pockets.

They were now street creatures of Madrid's northwestern suburbs, and they were hungry.

12:30 h

The table in the Serrano-Navas family's kitchen seated four, but at it there had always been room for Ethan. His spot was by the window, and from there he had an excellent view of Taberna de Regiones, a close second to Botín as his favorite restaurant. Their sautéed sliced potatoes drizzled with garlic mayonnaise and tomato sauce were one of his favorite *tapas*: Spain's tasty hors d'oeuvres.

Those house potatoes were one of the few foods he had never "spoiled," as Rebeca put it, with even a dot of hot sauce. His longtime friend Óscar was hosting a dinner at Taberna on Sunday for employees of his start-up media corporation, including INFOradio, for which Ethan was its U.S. correspondent. House potatoes would be the perfect beginning to his last night.

Fighting back a yawn, Ethan glanced at the clock. He was comforted by the early hour and the difference between how his native and adopted cultures described that time of day: *It's early afternoon back home, but here it's just late morning*. Whichever way he referred to it, he had at least an hour until lunch. He returned to the items lying on the placemat, including an unusually meager pile of change, at which he could not help smiling.

One- and two-euro coins were as popular in the European Union as one-dollar coins were unpopular in the United States. Despite Rebeca's and María Luisa's helpful nudges and reminders, when it came to making small purchases, Ethan was accustomed to paying with paper. One- and two-euro coins often languished in his pocket: forgotten victims of his American conditioning to fractional change (pennies, nickels, dimes, quarters).

But he had been conscientious this trip, and his pile of change was small. Rebeca would be proud. María Luisa, too, but their pats on the back would have to wait.

He turned his attention again to the fan of small bills. Forty euros, plus the six in change, were enough to get him through if he continued to spend wisely. But always being good was beginning to make Ethan a dull boy. After a moment's hesitation, he picked up a sheet of paper folded into a makeshift wallet and tapped on it until his emergency credit card and last large bill slid out onto the table.

As he stared at them, wavering like a candle flame that could burn down a house, the expressions "*soltar la mosca*—cough up money" and "*guardar la mosca*—save money" crept into his mind.

He had learned the opposing colloquialisms while reading Ramón J. Sender's *La tesis de Nancy*, about the adventures of an American student doing doctoral research in Seville. Ethan's exchange studies adviser had bought him the novel while they and what had felt like a million Madrileños were dazzled by the Christmas sights along the Gran Vía, a lively and upscale "street that never sleeps," known as much for its shopping as for the lavish architecture of its tall buildings.

The memory of that Christmas, his first one away from home, triggered queasy thoughts about the coming one, the first one his mother would be "spending with the angels," as his aunt had put it. His gaze wandered out the window. He remained lost in a cocktail of emotions until the pragmatism he had inherited from his bean-counting father broke through: *Live within your abilities. Go home, work hard, come back. And listen to the tape.*

"Easy for Dad to say," Ethan whispered and then unfolded his paper wallet. The sheet was a photocopy of his passport, and he carried it instead of the actual document. Spanish law required him to carry legal documentation at all times, but unless he was cashing a check or venturing outside the autonomous Comunidad de Madrid, he with his slate blue eyes and unremarkable blond hair felt better knowing the original was in Rebeca's lockbox. *Don't forget to get that back from her.*

The reminder was tinged with grayness, but he refused to brood and turned his attention back to the paper. "What a horrible picture," he said with a wince, checking the expiration date. *I'll be glad when it's time to get a new one.*

If Ethan stuck to his routine, in two years the passport would be another souvenir, replaced by one with a new headshot with which he would find the same old faults. But Óscar's start-up had yet to see the black side of the ledger. Until it did, Ethan would only get "attaboys!" for his night-owl radio broadcasts, so he relied on his job at the library and occasional checks from Mom and Dad to fund his hops across the pond. With Dad approaching retirement and Mom about to spend her first Christmas with the angels . . .

He began to pick at his cuticles.

"Jackass," he chided himself. *Didn't Mom's death teach you anything? Yes, you're going home on Monday; live for today—go to the BurgoCentro, buy some candy.* He refolded the copy and poked the contents back inside. *I'll do a little window-shopping, too*, he decided as he tucked the paper into his back pocket and buttoned it.

Rebeca had spotted the perfect box for his mom's tape that morning, but he felt bad for not having been the person to find it. *Funny how the first one often ends up being the one.* He gathered the coins and let them fall into his front pocket. He then neatly folded the small bills and shoved them into the other pocket. "Forty euros," he lamented, sliding in his chair on the spotless terra-cotta. *The exchange rate was so much better with the peseta.*

His stocking feet skated toward the back of the apartment, where he knocked on the door across the hall from Rebeca's. The response was delayed.

"Come on in, my dear." Sra. Navas was sitting on the bed with a prayer book in her lap.

"Sorry to interrupt you," Ethan said, using the familiar form of address, "but I'm going to walk to the BurgoCentro. Do you need anything?"

"Yes, some decent guindilla peppers: The ones at the farmers market were hard."

"I'll see what I can find. And *I'm* paying."

"When frogs grow fur," Sra. Navas said with a determined smile. "Grab some money out of my purse."

Ethan wasn't going to win this conversation. He never did. "See you at two o'clock."

"Careful crossing," she worried as he closed the door.

He knew the traffic circle well. It had been the only dicey part of his long walk to and from Instituto Las Rozas I, or *El Instituto*, as most folks called it. Although he had crossed the intersection countless times, he was still grateful for Sra. Navas's concern. She was the only mother he had left.

He skated to the front of the apartment and slipped into the well-worn loafers beside his bed. "I'm working on it, Mom," he whispered, tapping the carry-on with his foot. He then shuffled into the *salón*, living room, where he rattled the purse on the table but did not open it.

He passed through the open French doors into the front hallway. *Good to go*, he told himself, glancing at the key-wound clock on the wall. The short pendulum's back-and-forth pace never seemed to change, but time was passing more quickly than he would have liked. *Don't you freakin' dare.*

13:00 h

Ethan survived the traffic circle and hopped onto the sidewalk in front of the BurgoCentro.

The three-level mall had grown as Las Rozas had, and the original building was connected to its newer reflection across the street (BurgoCentro II) by a covered footbridge. Its construction had displaced the third-floor boutique in which his host mother had earned spending money in the evenings; Ethan didn't miss either of them.

Gone, too, was the drive-through pizzeria. The game room with miniature bowling had made way for the expansion of Burger King: Spaniards were increasingly wolfing down fast food. But the places of which Ethan had so many happy memories were still there: the candy store, the bookshop, the grocery, despite the brick milk and the Krispis. The trees in the atrium were taller.

Down on the right, past *el parking*, was the park in which he had made a name for himself once he learned the subtleties of the dirt basketball court. On the left, BurgoCentro II had no park, and that was fine with him.

Avoiding the doggy landmines dotting the corner, he continued toward the side entrance, which was shaded by the footbridge. It had been a month since its awning had sheltered anyone from anything but the sun. *Lord, it's dry.* He slipped between two cars queued up for Whoppers and patatas fritas.

On the sidewalk, he paused to glance at the Sierra de Guadarrama, the mountain range to the north. *Relief may be in sight, though. Come on, Mother Nature, but in moderation, please.*

Spanish drivers cannonball along in any weather, so he was hoping for a gentle soaking that wouldn't flood the parched Meseta or complicate the drive to the airport on Monday morning. But with María Luisa behind the wheel, he would buckle up and hold on tight, rain or shine.

The doors swished open. Ethan stepped inside.

As his eyes adjusted, they were drawn to the booths ringing the freestanding elevator, and he smiled. *A craft fair.* He walked forward. A nod to a woodworker waxing turned bowls, a smile for a sculptor selling religious statues and figurines. *There still might be a better box for Mom's tape here somewhere.* He passed another booth and then stopped in front of a clothes rack from which hung airplanes fashioned out of empty soda cans. Their propellers crept in circles in the whisper of an old fan. On the end were two Fanta *Limón* biplanes.

Limón was a classic soft drink made with real lemon juice that Ethan had become addicted to during his first trip to Spain. Although the glass from that eight-ounce bottle had been recycled into many things, the label remained a cherished souvenir, slightly yellowed but crisp and clean under plastic in an album, along with dozens of other memory-evoking stubs, clippings, and photos.

"The planes are yours for fifteen euros," the peddler told Ethan, who responded with a vague shake of the head, and kept looking. "I can let you have them for fourteen."

"That's a good price," Ethan said, becoming dismayed as the man stood up. "But I need to look around before I buy anything. If I buy anything."

The man pushed harder. "I'd take thirteen."

"I'm tempted, but there isn't room in my suitcase. I doubt they'd make it home in one piece, even if there were."

"They're well made."

"I see that, but—"

The man reached under the table. "One for eight euros. I'll wrap it up tight in this box, and you can carry it on."

"Be my luck, I'll have to open it at *control de seguridad*, and the tape won't hold again."

The man began to tuck one flap under the next. "Do them this way, and the box will stay closed if those bastards make you open it."

"Thanks for the tip, but I was really looking for something for my mother."

"They make interesting gifts. What's her favorite soda?"

"Mom didn't drink soda," Ethan said, retreating, "but thanks again. If nothing else catches my eye, I'll be back. Good luck."

"Come on, man. I'm sure you have the money to help a guy out."

Ethan would never win the war against self-doubt or guilt-provoking noes, but this battle was his. He nudged an empty baby carriage out of the way. "Mom, God rest her soul, didn't like carbonated drinks or pushy people. So I've changed my mind and won't be back." He walked away, wearing an anxious grin as his heart pounded.

"*¡Adiós y hasta nunca, gilipollas!*"

"Goodbye and good riddance," Ethan said with twitching lips, echoing the man's words but omitting the *jerk*.

The man hurled another insult, but it drowned in a toddler's playful shrieks as Ethan dodged through the new play area. An entertaining island of primary colors in a sea of white tile and glass storefronts. With so many hard surfaces, the screams echoed loudly into Ethan's bad ear. *Damn infection.*

The microorganisms had invaded during his only year of college, and then overstayed their welcome. He still wondered if the specialist's excruciating suction hadn't actually led to his slight hearing loss and hypersensitivity to certain sounds. Whichever the cause, he tried to avoid loud places.

Ethan's heart was beating normally as he entered the atrium. He glanced fondly at the mishmash of coin-operated, kiddie rides.

The racing car he and Rebeca and then he and María Luisa had once wedged themselves into beepbeeped for attention. The once high-pitched, peppy horn was dull and sluggish. *We've all gotten older*, Ethan thought as he approached the car. It beepbeeped again, calling for a rider and a coin. Ethan had the coin, but he would have looked ridiculous riding alone. If his Spanish sisters had been with him, he would have felt slightly less ridiculous, but the awkwardness would have spoiled any memories they could have made.

He had no doubt that Rebeca would have tugged him inside the car with her again. But he and María Luisa, whose figure had widened since his exchange stay, would never have fit. *What would I do if she were here right now?* he asked himself. His fingertips were sweaty as he tapped them on the car. *What would I do if they were both here?* That question made him even more anxious than the first one, but as his eyes wandered, he shook off the thought: *I don't have to answer those questions, however. If I did, this is what I'd do.* He gave the car a gentle pat and headed for the candy store to buy his favorite lime-and-cola candies.

If Rebeca and María Luisa had been with him, he would have offered to buy them something, too. But today, he was alone, as he had been on those mind-clearing walks during his exchange stay. His host mother used to scold him for becoming *imposible* after depressing calls from his natural mother, and then bristled when he left to be by himself. He had had no contact with his host mother or her cock of a husband since leaving six years ago. He had thought about them: *Do they still live in that piso? Are they still married? Are they still alive?* And though he was back in Las Rozas, he had made no effort to get the answers to those questions.

They can't peck at me or kick me out this time. Dad can't tell me to come home to start applying for college, and Mom can't . . .

Ethan's pace slowed as his mind raced. Guilty feelings were provoking him back to the craft fair: *If I can't make myself listen to Mom's tape, the least I can do is find a box to put it in.*

He stopped and turned around. The Fanta Limón biplanes were tinny specks. The peddler's booth was unattended.

Ethan sighed. *Well, I can't avoid him if I don't know where he—* A figure strolled out of the elevator and returned to the booth carrying what looked like a large cup. A few swigs, a fiery dot, puffs of smoke. The man sat down and then stood up as someone pushing a baby carriage passed the booth. Their words were beyond Ethan's earshot, but their Spanish gesticulations were within his view and comprehension: waving fingers up and down in front of the eyes—*I'm broke*; pretending to hold a small object and twisting it about—*do you get it?*; tapping the palm against the cheek—*you're shameless*; chopping the air with the hand—*you're gonna get it.*

Ethan shook his head. *The box can wait a little while longer.* He turned back around and headed for his sweet haunt for the second time during this visit to Las Rozas.

He moseyed inside, savoring the moment before focusing on a bin filled with tiny, sugar-coated, green-and-brown, bottle-shaped gummies. They were in a different place than they had been during his exchange stay, but the store was just as colorful and exciting: a rainbow explosion of candies, bins, jars, scoops, small bags and tubs. The large popper and bags of gourmet popcorn hanging near the register were new. So were the balloons and the tank of helium. And today, unlike a week ago, the familiar face of the owner was smiling at him from behind the counter.

"Good heavens," the woman said. "You're a sight for sore eyes. How long has it been?"

"Six years."

She looked Ethan up and down, almost wistfully, like a grandmother who was both proud and sad that her grandson had grown up. "You left as a boy and came back as a man," she said, gesturing that he had gotten taller and broader. "And handsome."

Ethan didn't believe her, but he blushed.

"And still shy."

He nodded. "But you haven't changed a bit," he lied. A gentle lie:

Her hair was whiter, her face more wrinkled.

"And you're still a sweet tooth."

"Oh, I'll always have a taste for my favorite little candies."

"Thank heaven for that," she said joyfully. "They're over there now."

Ethan didn't need to look where she was pointing. "I saw that you'd moved them when I was here last week. But I didn't see you then."

The woman patted her chest. "Having some health problems," she said with a frown and then quickly returned to talking about her store. "Moving things around keeps the store feeling fresh and new."

Ethan nodded again.

"What do you think about the new arrangement and the new popcorn? Oh, and the balloons?"

Ethan, who didn't think well on his feet, took a moment to answer: "This place feels like an old friend who's wearing new clothes."

"Well said," she told him as a boy scurried through the door towing his mother. "Excuse me for a moment," the owner told Ethan before turning to the excited little one. "Back for another balloon?" she asked him.

Ethan walked toward the bins and grabbed a scoop and a small, plastic tub. The pleasant plumps of his favorite candies against the bottom of the container were lost in the hissing of the helium tank and the squealing of the little boy's balloon. Ethan shook the tub, filled it, and reached for a lid. The lids were blue; they used to be clear, like the tubs. *Some things change, some things don't.*

He took a deep, cleansing breath and closed the lid.

13:45 h

The sun-touched handle burned into the creases of Thomas's fingers as he rattled the nave door of the Iglesia de San Miguel. He had heard the latch engage, but a part of him needed further convincing, and he couldn't bring himself to let go despite the pain.

A silver-haired man shuffled around the corner. "For heaven's sake, enough already!" he shouted.

Shock and embarrassment forced Thomas's hand off the iron.

"The door . . . has swollen in the sun. It's sticking."

The old man said nothing but continued forward.

Deflecting the man, Thomas rubbed his fingertips. "The handle's hot, so be careful."

"The heat gets more stubborn every year," the man said, stopping to wipe his brow with a pressed handkerchief. "My grandson says it's our fault . . . the global warming."

"Global warming?"

The man stared at Thomas's pale skin. "I blame *los moros*."

Thomas wondered what Muslims from northern Africa had to do with the rise in global temperatures, but he was happy to continue turning the conversation. "The moros?"

"There are just too many of them, and now they're invading this country, this continent, probably yours, too. When the sun's rays hit their dark skin, they get absorbed and can't reflect back into space. Everything heats up."

Thomas had spoken to the old man in passing a few times before. He lived in the Regiones neighborhood and walked the church grounds wearing a blue, V-neck cardigan and a red driving cap—disturbing reminders of the uniform worn by post-Civil War fascists during the 1940s. He appeared to Thomas to be mildly retarded or to have had a stroke, but Marisa's mother said he was just a curmudgeon who had been poky for as long as she had known him.

"Well, I'm waiting for someone," Thomas lied. "Have a good walk."

"I will. There aren't any moros in my way."

Again with the moros? Thomas thought.

"They're infidels and would never set foot in a church of the true faith until after dark."

Thomas sighed deeply. His deflection had succeeded—if the provocation of blatant racism could be considered a success. "After dark?"

"Burglary. Vandalism. They use the cover of night to avenge *la Reconquista*."

Thomas was perplexed, but not by the familiar history: In 1492, nearly eight hundred years after the Moors invaded the Iberian Peninsula, the expansion of Christian kingdoms toward Moorishcontrolled territory—the Reconquest—ended when the last Moorish king surrendered Granada to the army of King Ferdinand II and Queen Isabella I.

In the man's assertion that North African Muslims were now rafting across the Strait of Gibraltar to loot Christian churches (they were actually fleeing poverty, hunger, and war), Thomas sensed the rumblings of fascism and Franco; in his casting of blame on the moros for global warming, Thomas heard Nazism and the führer. He bit his tongue.

"Fernando II de Aragón—"

"I'm going," Thomas said, aborting the lesson, and glanced at the door as he turned. "I'll be sure to tell any moros to stay out of your way."

The man snorted into his handkerchief. "See you soon."

The hell you will, even if Marisa gets her wish.

But she wouldn't get her wish, not really. There was a way for him to stay a little longer, but the use of "force," though not out of the question, was consequential. But even if he could muster up the courage, he wouldn't be *with* her, not in the way she desperately wanted.

And he wouldn't be *with* Lina, not now, not ever, not even if he tried another drug and kept taking it despite the side effects. He was more damaged than anyone but Marisa knew, and it was only a matter of time until he was found out. *What would they say if they saw me getting ready to go away?*

Thomas hated going away, and when he did step outside the apartment back home in the States, the "out-the-door" routine could take hours, even for simple trips to the store. Preparations for weekend getaways could take days. Vacations tasked him for weeks, but they were worth it, at least the going. The chronic OCD that suffocated him at home became acute when he was away, and he could "breathe," shallowly. But as the return to rented hell loomed, his breathing labored, and he gasped.

Traveling by car was difficult: putting the car in first gear or reverse four times, rattling the locked door handle seventeen times. Negotiating airports and flights was worse. From the ticket counter to the security checkpoint to the seat on the plane, everyone was in a hurry. Rushing imbued him with anxiety, and he checked, rechecked, and re-rechecked the travel documents, the carry-on, the seatbelt, the tray table. Some zipper, buckle, or latch would linger in his memory as he stared out the window, unwilling to sleep. Time would pass too quickly if he fell asleep, and he would be home, in prison.

Whether he was the warden, the inmate, or both, there was an unhealthy comfort to home once he settled back into his routines. Settling back, however, required getting back inside the apartment. Anxious and resigned to self-incarceration, he trudged toward the door, where he lingered: Inching the key into the lock always took more courage than he could muster on the first attempt.

Eventually, he made it inside and to the recliner, in which he could sit for hours, staring at the baggage he had just "correctly" placed in front of the couch that no one had sat on for years. More often than not, he slept where he fell, curled in depression with his head on the arm of the recliner until the nightmare of transitioning from life out of a suitcase to obstacles like dresser drawers and closet doors startled him awake—

The old man doubled his handkerchief and grabbed the iron. The door opened and closed easily. "You were up to no good, or your brain is no good. Which one is it?"

Thomas hadn't made it back to the bench; he needed to get back to the bench. He tugged on the bracelet around his wrist and then turned. "Pardon?"

"I didn't have any problem with the door."

"Well, I did."

"No one who heard your infernal rattling doubts that."

"Sorry I had trouble with it. My fault, *Generalísimo.*" Thomas gave him a crisp, one-finger salute. "Again, I'll tell any moros to stay out of your way." He spun on his heels and headed for the shadow of the plane tree.

"*¡Insolente!* General Franco, God rest his soul, was a great man. He's not to be mocked, nor I."

"Señor," Thomas shouted over his shoulder, "you need to be getting home before another boat lands, and it gets even hotter."

The man rattled the door. "Or were you trying to loosen it for those thieving moros? Maybe you're their accomplice."

Thomas stopped.

"I bet back in America you have black friends. I haven't seen you with any here, but I bet you do." He pointed his handkerchief toward the bench. "Does that girl you meet over there know that?"

Thomas tugged four more times on the knot.

"I doubt she would look at you the same way if she did. Her poor mother."

A brazen puff drifted across the sun, but it wasn't a dip in temperature that made the hairs on Thomas's arm stand on end. *Goddamned OCD.* He rubbed his finger across the ridge beneath the bracelet, and turned back. "Señor, to offend you or your sensibilities was not my intention." He stepped toward the man, hand extended. "Let us goes, go our separate ways and end a conversation that should never have begun."

"Go back to your waiting . . . and your black friends. I'm not shaking that hand, not—"

"What the hell do you want from me?" Thomas barked. "So I rattled the damn door; not my first time, not my last. I'll prostrate myself on Franco's tomb the next time I visit the Valle de los Caídos. Will *that* make you happy?"

"The Valley of the Fallen, a grand monument to those who fell for God and Spain."

Built by political prisoners who "redeemed" themselves by creating a monument that was supposed to honor thousands of war dead, but only the names of Franco and his fascist buddy appear on it. Thomas gave the knot another tug. "A fitting tribute," he said. "I look forward to seeing it again, but not today."

"The memorial cross is the tallest one in the world—"

"I've stood at the base of it several times."

"The basilica is larger than Saint Peter's in Rome—"

"I have no reason to doubt you." Thomas glanced at the bench.

"The architect—"

"Or to continue bothering you," Thomas said in retreat. "Again, sorry about the door."

The old man shuffled after him. "The architect—"

"Señor, I must be getting back."

"The architect—"

"Enough," Thomas said, glaring at the handle. He thought of a distant doorknob and a dull blade in a toolbox. And cowardice. And hell. "For the rattling of that door I have done my penance," he vented; "you have seen to that." He stepped forward. "But the lesson is over—"

Four cookie-cutter *chavales*, kids, topped the nearby steps and ambled toward the stand of trees in the corner.

"The lesson is over," Thomas repeated, "as my visit soon will be." He watched the foursome plop down onto the picnic table. On it were scratched two names that Marisa had inscribed with a heart. Before the seats of the kids' Red Tab Levi's could warm the wood, the gang was puffing on cigarettes. *Spaniards are born with nicotine-stained fingers*, Thomas thought.

His mind then leapt back to the handle, the clank of the latch, and the singe of the iron. But he managed to focus on the old man: "Underage smokers . . . lawbreakers . . . who live under your nose must certainly be more worrisome than a door rattler from far away. Go talk to them."

"In time."

"There's no time like the present," Thomas said. "And since I'm going home on Monday—"

"Thank goodness."

"And 'thank goodness' this conversation is over. Again, I apologize for my 'infernal rattling.' Goodbye. Good luck. Have a nice life, what's left of it." Thomas dug his toe into the gravel and cut a line as he spun to go. "Have a nice afterlife, too," he smirked. "If you think it's hot now, you infernal fool, wait until you get to Hell. Say hello to Franco for me."

14:15 h

Lentils with chorizo, carrots, and celery had been one of Rebeca's favorite dishes for as long as she could remember, but today she had no appetite for sitting down to a family lunch. Lingering on her family's balcony, she plucked two peppermint leaves, crushed them, and held them to her nose. The aroma bit at her nostrils, and her eyes teared again.

She hated leaving Álvaro to brood in the gazebo, and though she regretted *how* the conversation ended, in light of her last confession, *why* it ended seemed far more regrettable.

The priest had spoken of prudence and temperance, and she had expected Álvaro's grandmother to buttress his case for abstinence. To Rebeca's dismay, the two old souls were like holy oil and execrable water, the former counseling her to gain God's favor by resisting temptations of the flesh, the latter insisting that she would not be damned for giving herself to a man if she did so honestly. The key was "honestly," and to help her understand what she meant by it, Álvaro's grandmother had asked her a wickedly simple question: "Have you ever sinned against a rose?" The explanation replayed in Rebeca's head:

"Sinned against a rose? No. Is that even possible?"

"Have you ever picked one?"

"I picked the ones Mamá used to grow. She took great pride in them. We floated the flowers in a bowl of water on the kitchen table as a centerpiece."

"Have you ever stolen one from someone else? A store? A neighbor?"

"Papá tells the story of me plucking one from a pot outside Café Sol. It was a rare variety. One of the waiters gave Papá a real talking-to, and then Papá gave me one about not touching things. It was a big to-do, but it wasn't stealing."

"Why not?"

"Because I was little and couldn't read the sign."

"What if you had been older, old enough to know right from wrong?"

"That would have been stealing, in the eyes of the law and God."

"Let's set crimes aside; man's laws and God's laws aren't always in harmony. Would it have been a sin?"

"Yes. 'Thou shall not steal.'"

"Would it have been a sin to steal one of your mother's?"

"I was allowed to take them, so no."

"Would it have been a sin to damage one of them by accident?"

"No, but if I had lied about it, yes."

"Say she had grounded you for missing curfew, and to spite her you broke a few stems but admitted to doing it. Would *that* have been a sin?"

"I did something like that once, but it was about a boy. I picked the most beautiful flower and crushed it with my foot. I guess it was a sin: 'Obey thy father and thy mother.'"

"And was the picking and the crushing a sin?"

"I'm still not sure you can sin against a flower."

"Do you remember how it felt to crush it?"

"Perversely pleasing. I felt bad afterward, though."

"How were you feeling as you reached to pick it?"

"Vengeful," Rebeca said anxiously.

"Did you like that feeling?"

"Not really. That's not me."

"Did it feel wrong?"

"Yes."

"But you did it anyway."

"It was just a rose."

"*What* it was isn't the point; that you picked it when it felt wrong to do so *is*. That's the sin."

Rebeca frowned. "What if it hadn't felt wrong?"

"But it did."

"Some things I do feel wrong, but they aren't."

"Such as?"

"I just told Álvaro that I want to move far away."

"And do you?"

"With all my heart," Rebeca said, resisting the urge to fidget.

"What's your inner voice telling you?"

"That what I want to do is the right thing. And it's more than a want; I need to do it, I have to do it, like breathing."

"And you're not lying to me to justify doing it?"

Rebeca shook her head emphatically: "No."

"Are you lying to yourself?"

"I lie to myself a lot, but not this time. I know the difference."

"So telling my grandson the truth *felt* wrong, I suppose, because you were making a mess of his plans. You were spoiling his vision of starting your life together in that piso you looked at the other day."

"He has a steady job here, working for Papá. Majadahonda's practically next door. He could walk to work if he had to."

"But your heart and mind are somewhere else."

"I keep thinking of what happened to Ethan's mother," Rebeca said. "Dead in just three months."

"Death has a funny way of making us stare into the mirror and then changing how we feel about the reflection."

"I don't like what I see," Rebeca said. "There's too much I've been afraid to do."

"Like having sex? Pregnancy, sexually transmitted diseases—"

"Those things aren't the reason I haven't had sex. It's just never felt right."

"And now it does?"

"In every fiber of my being. It's time."

"Not if you're feeling guilty, it isn't, or if you're compromising in order to get what you want. Virginity isn't an honest commodity, no matter what . . ."

A driver pounded out a series of angry honks. The shrillness was too much for even a horn addict like Rebeca to ignore. She balled the crushed leaves, popped the mint into her mouth, and blotted her eyes with her sleeve: a handy tissue for a girl who didn't wear makeup.

The moving truck that had been circling the block was now double-parked down the street, exasperating one of Rebeca's neighbors, a woman built like a fireplug with bleached hair as big as her salty mouth. She frequented Sr. Serrano's taberna. Her drink of choice was anisette, and according to Álvaro, she chose it early and often. She laid on the horn again and then pried herself out of the car to rip into a man in coveralls.

This should be good, Rebeca chuckled, unaware that Ethan was also watching the scene.

Let the games begin, he quipped, his tongue picking at bits of lime-and-cola candy stuck in his teeth as he continued to wait to cross Avenida de la Constitución. Except for dregs of sugar, the small tub in his hand was empty. He burped it one last time and dropped it into a plastic bag with a few guindillas. After fixing his socks, he checked left and right. Uncharacteristically late for being early but in no particular hurry, he let a truck clatter past and then crossed, still wondering why his Spanish sister's daydream had gone bad. "Hey, guapa!" he shouted. "Done spacing out?"

Flushing, Rebeca began to rewrap her ponytail. "Just watching the show."

"Entertaining, but it's not enough to bring *me* to tears," he teased.

"I'll give you something to cry about," she joked huskily and spat the mint at him.

"Your aim is as bad as your cooking. Guess I'll have to save my tears for Monday."

"No tears here. I'll be glad to see you go," she said with a wink. "And so will the stores around here: I hear they're running out of change."

Slapping his pocket, Ethan managed a wry smile. "You heard wrong."

"Impressive."

"I've done well, but with two well-intentioned nags like you and your sister, how could I not?"

"I'll take 'well-intentioned,' but another word comes to mind when I think of my sister."

Ethan stepped closer. "She's the only one you've got, and you never know for how long." His eyes were glistening. "Life's short. Be nice."

Rebeca could see the pain on his face. She leaned over the balcony. "I'm very sorry about your mother."

"Thank you," he whispered.

"And I'll try to be nice, ¿*vale?*"

"*Vale,*" Ethan said.

He loved that ubiquitous, little "okay." It brought back memories of the start of his exchange studies, when the first and last words of sentences were the only ones he caught. How he, someone who could conjugate hundreds of irregular verbs flawlessly and knew three words for *pea*, could have been so lost still amazed him.

Far less amazing were the insults boiling out of the woman down the street: "¡*Subnormal!* ¡*Troglodita!*" Ethan had heard those from his host parents. Any chance of learning a new *taco*, swearword, drowned in the loud beeps of the truck's back-up alarm.

The two watched the fireplug plop down into the driver's seat and slam the door. The car dragged to a start.

"She's a lively one," Rebeca said. Her mind and then her gaze wandered down to the Plaza Mayor. The chess tournament had ended, and preparations for tonight's concert were underway. Her caramel eyes brightened.

"Lively?" Ethan said. "Another word comes to mind."

No response.

"Rebeca?"

"Yes?"

"I said that another word comes to mind."

"Now who needs to be nice?" Rebeca asked as the woman came off the clutch late and took off before the truck had finished backing up. Her noisy transmission increased in pitch as she approached.

Ethan winced. "Touché."

"You better get inside and save your ear for the concert."

He nodded. "I'm looking forward to it."

"Me, too. Tell Mamá I'll be in shortly."

"*Vale.*" He let a customer exit La Rinconera and then shuffled toward a set of narrow doors and rang the intercom. "It is I," he told María Luisa, who quickly buzzed him in, but before entering he paused. "Psst!"

Rebeca slipped between two pots and leaned on the railing.

"I promise to keep your leaky moment to myself, but if you need anything—"

"Tears of joy," she said. "Don't you worry."

"I guess anything's possible," he said, slapping his pocket, "but the offer still stands."

"I know."

He stepped inside and pulled the door closed. *She can talk the ears off a billy goat, but she's a horrible liar.* His tongue dug at the last bit of candy as he started up the stairs. *But what do I know?*

Outside, Rebeca was regretting the half-truths she had told. Poor, patient Álvaro. She considered herself an honest person, but like most she fibbed about little things (the scratch on the car, her aunt's new hairstyle). Mingling small lies with the honest truth that she wanted to give her virginity to the man she loved had seemed like the smart thing to do.

But sex was a big thing, the biggest, at least to her. When her feelings came to light, she wondered if they would see her as immature and unable to handle the emotions that came with being sexually active. But did it really matter how "they" saw her? For all "they" knew, she liked being Daddy's little girl. *Stop complicating the issue. Tell him.*

But in the telling lay the problem.

She could unblushingly broach the subject and then utter the words, of course; her Catholic upbringing hadn't stunted her that much. Unless she could keep herself from saying too much, he might doubt that he knew her at all. She knew him, though, even things he didn't realize that she knew, and now she wanted to "know" him, to make love and lie naked in his arms with her head on his chest. The fantasy made her nipples get hard. She crossed her arms, staring at the nave of the Iglesia de San Miguel.

The doors were scarlet like a torero's cape, but like a bull that had seen too many passes, she was wise to the deception and determined to sink herself into something real.

14:45 h

Sr. Serrano rarely had time to linger at the family lunch table. Today was no exception. He sopped up his lentils with the last slice of bread, forked a wedge of tomato and a sliver of onion from the platter of mixed salad, and took a slice of melon, which he ate with a knife. As he did, he took in the conversation taking place across the dining table in his comfortable salón. Rebeca's lips were moving, the boys were listening attentively, and María Luisa was rolling her eyes: All was well. After swigging his wine, he stood up. "I need you by five o'clock," he told his future son-in-law.

"Of course," Álvaro said, managing to tear his eyes off Rebeca. His fiancée had found her smile. It seemed to be tinged with anxiety, or maybe it was eagerness, like a student about to start college, but she was smiling, and, damn, she was cute.

"Handle the soft drink delivery if I'm tied up with the electrician."

"*Vale.*"

María Luisa wiped her mouth. "The electrician?"

Sr. Serrano knew better than to be encouraged by his daughter's flash of interest in the taberna. "The damn circuit breakers keep tripping."

"I did a little research on the problem," Álvaro volunteered, "and based on what I read, we need a service with higher amperage."

"You may have to replace the panel and the meter if that's the case," Ethan added. "Maybe upgrade the wiring, too. That's a big job. And an expensive one."

Stopping short of the open French doors, Sr. Serrano nodded. "Let's hope not."

"*How* expensive?" Rebeca asked, her smile fading.

"We'll feel the pinch if Ethan's right, but these are things you have to do when you own a business, my daughter." He kissed Sra. Navas as she returned from the kitchen with a bottle of mineral water, and gave her a playful pat on the ass. Before opening the front door, he poked at his older daughter: "Not that *you'll* ever have to worry about something like owning a business, my head case."

María Luisa stabbed an olive and a bit of tuna, swirled them in vinegar, and shoved them in her mouth as her father left.

Sra. Navas sighed as she approached the table. She loved them both but hated it when they were together. "Water, anyone? Ethan, my dear, don't you need a little more to wash down that hot sauce?"

"I'm fine, thanks."

"He's used to the heat, Mamá," Rebeca said, "but *I* read . . . somewhere . . . that you can avoid jet lag on long flights by drinking a lot of water. Give him some more anyway. The boy needs to stay hydrated."

"The humidity in commercial aircraft is comparable to that in the Sahara," Álvaro explained. "It's also important to get up and move around the cabin to prevent blood clots."

Ethan was an experienced traveler but appreciated the concern. "Top it off," he said. "I've had my fill of doctors and hospitals."

Sra. Navas's eyes met María Luisa's. Ethan's Spanish mother placed one hand on his shoulder and with the other poured the water.

15:25 h

Formed at the meeting of Avenida Toreros and the steep Calle Maestro Alonso, the Plaza de España was a modern, pedestrian square with a resident population of pigeons that roosted in the arcades of the three-storied buildings that enclosed it on the north and west. Unlike Madrid's touristy Plaza Mayor, the shops underneath the arches catered to everyday life: a tobacconist, a fishmonger, an antique shop, two spaces for rent, a travel agency, an accountant, and on the end of the shorter, western arcade, the popular Café Sol, which sprawled out into the cobblestoned square in good weather.

A stone's throw from the Café's umbrella tables and in the center of the plaza stood a wooden gazebo with a thatched roof. Beyond the cobbles, across Avenida Toreros, was the Virgen de la Retamosa and her fountain.

A hike from both school and his host parents' piso, the Plaza de España hadn't been one of Ethan's regular haunts until the final days of his exchange stay, when he became a fixture at the Serrano-Navas family's table. And when he wasn't savoring a plate of pisto or helping Rebeca with her English assignments under the watchful eye of her meddling sister, "*El Rubio*—the Blond One," as the neighbors called him, hoofed it to the gazebo to watch the pigeons, especially the white ones, as conspicuous among their pale gray flock as Ethan was among his olive-complected kith and kin.

Perhaps on a subconscious level he identified with those birds, or maybe he wanted to: They were different *and* beautiful. But he knew they reminded him of his first trip to the peninsula, that cloudless morning in Seville among the white doves in the Parque de las Palomas (Dove Park). As is often the case with endings, he couldn't help thinking of beginnings.

But this afternoon he was pressed for time, and reminiscences and his birds would have to wait. The box that Rebeca had pointed out was on his mind. On the odd chance that the antique shop hadn't closed for the siesta, he had returned to the plaza to squeeze in some proper browsing before the bullfight, one of the few things in Spain, if not the only thing, that began on time. His loafers thumped across the cobbles.

To a vaguely familiar face at one of the tables he gave a typical nod of acknowledgment, got one in reply, and then continued on his way with a grin, feeling like one of the guys.

But the stranger who slithered out of the gazebo quickly made Ethan feel like an outsider. His blue eyes lost their brightness. His blond head fell. He shoved his hands into his pockets.

"You like bracelets?" the petty thief asked. His Andalusian accent was as thick as his clothing was dingy and his face was thin, but

Ethan had no trouble understanding him.

"Yes . . . but I—I don't need a bracelet."

The tall, dark-skinned rag stepped closer. "Are you sure?"

"No thanks. Not now."

"Later, then?"

"Not today."

"Come on, boy. *La' fiesta'* are over tomorrow." He slid forward. "What if I can't find you?"

"I'll find *you*," Ethan lied, taking a small yet hopeful step to the side.

The rag mirrored him. "Why wait?"

Ethan fumbled around in his pockets. "Now's not a good time. I need to do some shopping before the bullfight, so please excuse me." Even in terror he was polite.

Their eyes met briefly, but the rag had never taken his eyes off Ethan. He seized his prey by the elbow. "I killed a bull once," he boasted as his dirty fingernails dug into Ethan's sweater. "Do you know what a *maletilla* is?"

Despite the tingling sensation in his arm and his racing pulse, Ethan was uncharacteristically clear under stress: "A maletilla is a novice who tries to get famous by following the bulls and participating in amateur bullfights."

The rag was impressed but gave Ethan's elbow another squeeze. "The bullfighting world is an old-boy network that's almost impossible to break into. I had to practice at night, by moonlight. Ranchers don't take kindly to that kind of practice, but hunger makes you take horrible risks." He let go of Ethan's elbow. "And I did learn to handle a sword," he declared with a yellowed smile and a cock of the head. "Let me show you the blade I found. After you see the clean edges it leaves on the leather bracelets, I'm sure you'll change your mind—"

"I'll take two. How much?"

"For you, boy, five euros."

"Fine," Ethan exhaled. "One moment, please." He turned his back to the threat, let his Swiss army knife fall to the bottom of his pocket, and pulled out a neat fold of paper euros. He peeled off a sweaty five-euro banknote, unaware that the predator had sidled up to him.

"*Gracia'*," the rag said, snatching the bill before the word had escaped his lips. He slipped two bracelets into his startled customer's pocket with frightful ease.

"You're welcome," Ethan said insincerely, shoving his hands back into his pockets. His heel caught on a cobble as he began his retreat.

"A pleasure doing business with you, boy."

"Until forever," Ethan hoped. His eyes leapt from the rag's sneakers to the Iglesia de San Miguel. "Until forever. Please, God."

"Until later," the rag shouted, wearing a lordly grin that made Ethan hate himself even more. "With all that money in your pocket, we're sure to meet again." He slipped into the gazebo, grabbed a cosmetic case, and left.

15:50 h

Overcoming his inertia, Thomas centered a tube glass on its coaster and timorously stood up, grateful that none of Café Sol's feathered clients were underfoot as he pushed in the chair. The birds were taking a siesta, as were many Roceños, and they had missed the pitiful show at the gazebo. *Loser.* He nudged the glass slightly and tugged eight times at the leather around his wrist. *What a fucking loser.*

Staring at the slightest of blemishes in the gazebo's fresh paint—Thomas had keen eyes for "abnormalities" in his environment—he eased his hands into his pockets.

The bracelet twisted.

All was not well . . .

Deciding to leave just the leftover change as a tip, he neatly arranged the coins on the table and then untwisted the bracelet and tugged at its knot four times. *Sure wish I had brought that superglue,* he thought, picturing a perfectly placed tube in the apartment back in the States. He began to mull over ideas for the column he would write when he got back there.

But he didn't want to return to that hellish apartment, not now, not ever. His gaze fixed on the antique shop. *I might not have the nerve for it, but at least there is a way.*

16:00 h

The sun was relinquishing blue skies to a scattering of clouds, but the Plaza de España's street trees were still, as were Ethan's birds. Roosted in the arched passageways, they softly cried in that contented way pigeons do, cooing the plaza to sleep while Roceños with full bellies and late-night plans were at home getting their second wind.

The rag had gone, off to God knows where, with Ethan's money and a heaping of self-satisfaction. And Ethan, who was in no mood to sleep, had the northern arcade to himself. He was relieved to be alone. As he stood there watching the wispy cirrus clouds, he imagined that the afternoon had gotten away from him. Without a watch he couldn't be sure, and for the moment, he didn't care to find out.

With a sigh, he started toward the antique shop. It was an easy blink of a journey compared to his walk to the BurgoCentro on legs that had taken a beating during the encierro. But as he felt his bony knees roll inward, he questioned his decision not to spend the siesta relaxing. *Too late now.* He thought about each step, about each cycle of right then left, wondering how long it would be before he caught a toe. At least no one would see him if he did.

Passing the fishmonger, he spotted a handful of live crayfish in the window and paused to muse upon his first afternoon as an exchange student. He would never forget that bowl of live *cangrejos de río* in the refrigerator: They had given him such a startle. Those critters his host mother had stewed in tomato sauce, garlic, and onions, and he was sure that these were also doomed to have their red heads enthusiastically sucked.

But not by him. He had politely passed on that suggestion years ago, as he had a few days later when his host father offered him the rabbit's head. Delicacy or not, he had no interest in sucking the brain out of anything.

An unpalatable trip down memory lane began as brick milk, anisette, blood sausage, tripe, and fatty salt pork flashed through his mind. He could still see that bristly chunk of pig in his first plate of Asturian bean stew. But *fabada* was also made with chorizo, and at the thought of that spicy sausage he could not help smiling. With few exceptions, Spanish food had that effect on him. He would miss it; he had already begun to miss it. With a pang of anxiety, the box in the window leapt to mind.

He wished the crayfish luck, senselessly hoping that among a people obsessed with the tradition of the bullfight there was a merciful cook who would ice them before their hellish plunge, and then continued down the arcade.

His shadow deepened as he neared the antique shop. Antaño's display window glittered in the sun, and on the wall its brass nameplate shone, drawing Ethan's eye to a sheet of paper taped below it. The sign read *OJO, PINTA*—WET PAINT, and below the impeccable handwriting was an arrow that pointed toward the open doorway, which smelled of solvent. The warm weather was ideal for painting, but Ethan had had enough of summer.

Without lifting his pant legs, he adjusted the knotted socks while scratching a phony itch. When his pants were hanging straight, he shuffled forward, running his hand across one of the pillars supporting the arches. The building block was fine-grained granite. A former geology student, he preferred his rocks in the rough and found the manicured stone merely utilitarian. The shop's façade, however, drew him forward. Its diamond-paned window, wall-mounted vase with fresh-cut gerberas, and swaybacked threshold gave it a quaintness that invited him inside, as did Pachelbel's *Canon in D major*, playing softly.

He ducked a wind chime that a doorstop had rendered silent.

The shop was a skinny rectangle but uncluttered and bright despite the red clay floor tiles and coffered ceiling. The long wall onto which the door opened was covered with horizontal paneling that had a very European feel. Hanging perfectly level on it were various metal signs, two gilded mirrors, a small clock with a lifeless pendulum, and two oil paintings that needed to be cleaned.

To the left, the wall of shelves was pregnant with perfectly faced, small items, including bronzes, lamps, tins, toys, and vases. A lighted display counter ran from front to back, and then turned ninety degrees and stopped.

On the other side of the narrow pass-through, the jewelry

counter ran to the paneled wall, and on it sat the cash register, the paraphernalia of transacting business, and a burning jasmine-scented candle.

And in back were two floor-to-ceiling cabinets, a small table with a bookshelf stereo system and a neat stack of compact discs, and a curtained opening, from which an unassuming saleswoman appeared a few moments later as Ethan eyed an assortment of antique doorknobs.

"Sorry, I didn't hear you come in," she said, addressing him formally.

"*No hay problema.* I was just looking."

She glided toward the display counter. As she did, the coil of keys around her wrist jingled. "At anything in particular?"

"These doorknobs," Ethan said, tapping on the counter with his fingertip. The nail was cut far too short to reach the glass first.

"Would you like to see one?"

"Please."

Nodding, the saleswoman removed her wrist coil, selected the correct key with barely a hesitation, and unlocked the case. "Which one?"

"The swirled glass one."

"The art glass is quite beautiful, isn't it?" She handed him the knob.

"Very. It's heavier than I expected," Ethan said, appreciating the weight of the flattened sphere. From conversations with his mother about the lead crystal punch bowl and pitcher that had adorned the fireplace mantle until the divorce, he associated heavy glass with look-but-don't-touch decoration, but the weighty spheroid he was cradling was the epitome of artistry with a purpose.

For a turning doorknob, its size was ideal, at least for Ethan's hand. Inside the bright rind of clear glass, a central drop of orange tinged with pink melted into a short, lonely eddy of yellow and circular currents of blues, purples, and reds that filled half the depth of the knob. The back half was clear glass that rounded down to a thick stem, which fit inside a patinated collar with a square hole on the end. Ethan carefully probed the opening for sharp edges, turned the knob over, and began to rotate it between his palms.

"It's antique, probably from the nineteen twenties or thirties," the saleswoman said, watching him. "The mount is bronze, and there's no back plate or spindle."

Ethan's eyes sparkled. "I didn't come to buy a doorknob."

"You're the second person who has looked at it this afternoon. We have just that one."

"I came to look at the small box in the window," he said, hesitant to put down the knob; the swirls were mesmerizing. "I wasn't sure you'd be open."

"We usually close during the siesta, but we just varnished the door, and it's still wet."

"I saw the sign. Is that your handwriting?"

"Yes."

Ethan continued to turn the knob. "You have beautiful handwriting."

"Thank you."

"I get a lot of compliments on my cursive," Ethan said humbly with a shrug of his shoulders, "but I think it looks like a woman's. I've always been able to print like a typewriter, though. When I took drafting in *high eschool*, my teacher used to say that if he hadn't seen it with his own eyes, he would have sworn I had used a template." Caught between a frown and a smile at the thought of those simple yet trying years and the nearly impossible ones that followed, he glanced at the display window and back at the doorknob, which he now held tightly between his moist fingertips. "Printing is on the short list of things I do really well."

"Make sure speaking Spanish is on that list," the saleswoman said as he began to rotate the knob again. "You've acquired an impeccable accent."

"As my language teacher at El Instituto told me, 'You have to run many miles with a language to become familiar with it.'"

"Well, you certainly have run the miles."

Nearly lost in the swirls of color, Ethan was slow to acknowledge the compliment. "Thank you. A lot of miles. And a lot of help and patience from the locals."

"Roceños aren't xenophobic, and I think we're very welcoming to foreigners, especially those who want to assimilate."

Adagio for Strings melted to an end and the overture to Rossini's *The Barber of Seville* burst from the silence.

"That's been my experience," Ethan agreed, ignoring the faint faces of his host parents, which haunted his memory like ghostly images burned into a damaged computer display. Another face and another memory followed, one of helplessness and regret. His mind began to wander.

"I can show you the box if you'd like."

"Yes. Yes, please."

The saleswoman waited patiently for him to relinquish the knob, and then returned it to its place on the shelf and locked the case. "The other gentleman who looked at it said he might be back tomorrow morning," she added, gliding toward the front of the shop. "If you change your mind, we'll be open until nine o'clock. Or I can hold it for you."

"I don't think so, but how much is it?"

Quickly selecting another key, she smiled: "The price is twelve euros." She unlocked the display window and turned back to Ethan with the wooden box in her hand.

Not quite sixteen dollars, he told himself, a bit surprised. "Only twelve euros?"

"For you the price is twelve euros," the saleswoman said.

Ethan nodded appreciatively. "Thank you. It's *precioso*, but I really came for *that*," he repeated as he took the box from her and began to examine it. "My Spanish sister pointed this out to me while we were waiting for this morning's encierro to start. It's nice to finally put my hands on it."

It, too, was heavier than he expected, and in size and shape reminded him of a case for displaying an autographed baseball but not a softball. The square sides were joined with finger joints: a strong yet aesthetic woodworking joint that resembled two square-toothed combs interlocked at ninety degrees. The hinges were neatly mortised into the back and carved top. As Ethan expected, the bottom was made of a secondary wood, but he was pleased to see that the small panel sat in a groove cut into all four sides instead of being held on with nails or glue. "What can you tell me about it?"

"Let's see," she began. "It's been in the shop for a few months. It's old, turn of the century, perhaps, but I can't be sure. The wood is olive, and the carving on the lid is an olive tree. The finger joints were cut by hand. There's no maker's mark. It's well made."

Ethan ran his fingers over the olive tree. "It's beautiful."

"Isn't it?" she agreed. "And the size?"

"The size is fine."

She turned to the wall behind her. "I may have something a little larger."

"Really, it's perfect."

"Are you sure?"

"Very," Ethan said, turning the box over and over in his hands. "My mother lost her incredibly short battle with cancer a few months ago, but she made me a tape. I've been looking for something to keep it in, and this is perfect. How much are you asking?"

"I'm sorry for your loss," the saleswoman said and then paused as two clocks chimed the half hour within a second of each other. "Sixteen euros."

He acknowledged her condolences with a slow bow of the head. "Sixteen euros?"

"And not one *céntimo* more."

"*Es . . . una ganga*—It's . . . a bargain." His occasional reluctance to use colloquialisms his host mother had taught him was admittedly ridiculous, but the hurt still lingered.

"Nice word," the saleswoman said without the slightest hint of condescension.

"I learned that one a long time ago. Is the time really four thirty?"

"Yes."

"*¡Jo—lín!*" Ethan euphemized, catching himself mid-expletive. "The afternoon is whizzing by." His words were tinged with wistfulness and irritation.

"It'll be time for the late-afternoon snack before you know it."

"And *los toros*."

"Are you going to the bullfight?"

"Yes, and if I were at home in Estados Unidos, I'd be running late," he said anxiously.

"No need to worry: You're in *España*."

"And happy to be here," Ethan said, distraction tempering his enthusiasm. "But there's no sense rushing, if you would hold this for me."

"Of course," she agreed before locking the display window.

"Thanks a lot."

"Don't mention it," she said, returning to the counter, where she paused with a gentle tap on the glass. "I need to take down your information. Excuse me for a moment."

He nodded and then watched her glide toward the register. As she picked up pen and paper, he reached to set Rebeca's find on the counter. The case's fluorescent tube bathed the cube in cool light, but Ethan nearly choked with emotion as his fingers slid down the finger joints before finally letting the box go.

"And when you return, you'll have more time to browse if you like."

"Absolutely."

The saleswoman clicked the pen. "I'll be happy to hold it for a few days. Monday, Tuesday?"

"Tomorrow, for sure."

"Very well," she said, flipping open a small notebook, and wrote *domingo*, Sunday, as Ethan watched with the same sense of amazement his drafting teacher must have felt while watching him. "We open at ten o'clock, close at two, and then reopen from five to nine. Let me have your name and a phone number if you'd like."

"My name is Ethan, E-T-H-A-N, and you can reach me at 6-3-7-77-17." He rubbed the erect hairs on the back of his neck. "I'm staying with a family on Avenida de la Constitución, and they're probably expecting me because even in España," he said, "*something has to start on time.*"

She tucked the note inside the box. "You're right."

He thanked her, and after a warm handshake began backpedaling toward the door. "You have a beautiful store. I'll see you tomorrow," he said with a glance at the display case.

"It's nice to finally put a face to the name. Give Carmen my best."

Wearing a quizzical expression, Ethan's pace slowed to a stop.

The saleswoman smiled. "I've known Carmen since María Luisa was a tadpole."

"Rebeca didn't mention it," Ethan said, taken aback. "Small world."

The woman's smile broadened. "I wasn't sure at first that you were the young man who stays with them. And not often enough, from what I hear."

Ethan sighed. "That family is the salt of the earth, especially Sra. Navas."

"She's a wonderful woman. Complex, warmhearted, *extremely* perceptive. She thinks the world of you."

"And I of her. Of all of them," he said, flushing. "But they might put me out if I'm late. Until tomorrow, when I'll have more time. Again, thank you."

"You're quite welcome. I look forward to talking to you again. Enjoy the bullfight."

Ethan put his finger to his lips as he turned to go. "Not nearly as much as I used to, but please don't say anything."

The saleswoman shook her head. "Not a word. Not a word about any of it."

16:45 h

Awed by the mounted *rejoneador*'s artistic control of both horse and bull, Sra. Navas preferred the equestrian *rejoneo* to the classic bullfight, but she couldn't pass up the opportunity to spend the afternoon with her kids. Ethan wasn't really her son, but he was as much a member of the family as any adopted child could ever have been. She and Sr. Serrano had always wanted to have three children, but God had other plans for Félix. She had stopped asking why.

Wondering what was keeping Rebeca was another pointless exercise.

"Mamá, let's go," María Luisa insisted, tapping her foot on the sidewalk as she glared into La Rinconera.

Sra. Navas shook her head. "*Tranquila.*"

"I don't want to relax. She knows we're waiting. I'm going in."

Sra. Navas sighed. "Ethan, dear, would you mind going to get Rebeca while I have a word with my daughter?"

"Not at all," he said, already on his way. Grabbing the door, he mouthed "behave" to María Luisa.

She shot him a look that sent him quickly inside.

The tables in the main part of the taberna were empty. At the bar, three regulars were engaged in a boisterous conversation, eating olives, drinking wine, gesticulating with cigarettes, and talking over each other the way that Spaniards do.

Sr. Serrano had just exhausted one side of a jamón serrano. He turned it over and tightened the fixtures on the ham stand. A well-clamped ham and a sharp ham knife were essential to carving the meat into short, thin slices. Only he could sharpen the flexible blade to his satisfaction, and as he touched it up with a sharpening steel, the fruit slot machine by the pay phone began to play a tune.

It sounded and smelled like Spain, but no Álvaro or Rebeca.

No, there they are, Ethan told himself.

The couple was sitting in a smaller, more intimate part of the taberna that Sra. Navas called "*El Acueducto*" because of the partition's resemblance to the enduring aqueduct bridge built by the Romans to carry water to the fortified town of Segovia.

Segovia boasted several historical monuments, including three of the five original gates in the wall that surrounded the city center and the Catedral de Santa María, a masterpiece of gothic architecture known as the *Dama de las Catedrales* (Lady of Cathedrals). Although Sra. Navas was a religious churchgoer, what drew her periodically to the old yet thriving city to the north of Las Rozas was her fascination with the Acueducto's dry-laid arches and pillars (the granite blocks were held together only by gravity) and her taste for the signature dish of a restaurant in the Roman marvel's shadow.

Opened originally in 1786 as an inn, Mesón de Cándido was famous throughout Spain for its Castilian hospitality and its *cochinillo asado*, roast suckling pig: The pork was so tender it was cut with the edge of the plate on which it was served. Both of Sra. Navas's attempts at cochinillo in her electric oven had been less succulent—"edible," as Sr. Serrano had put it. Ethan had never dined at Mesón, but like characters in Ernest Hemingway's *The Sun Also Rises*, he had lunched on suckling pig at Botín, the world's oldest restaurant. "The key to preparing great cochinillo is a two hundred-year-old, wood oven," Ethan had once told Sra. Navas, giving her a consolatory peck on the cheek. He had then thanked her for the effort and assured her that the tastiness of her cooking was surpassed only by her hospitality, which was second to none.

Álvaro would be a lucky man if Rebeca became like her mother. Reluctantly, Ethan approached them, softening the intrusion with humor. "Kiss him already, honey, or we'll be late."

"Tell María Luisa to stick it," Rebeca said. "We can hear her from here."

Álvaro was not amused. He let go of Rebeca's hand, stood up, and shoved in his chair. "Time to go to work," he lamented. "Enjoy the bullfight."

"With the way I'm feeling," Rebeca said, "I might jump into the ring with the *vaquilla*." (Releasing an almost two-year-old bull, vaquilla, into the ring after an encierro or bullfight was a popular tradition.) "See you after."

"*Vale*," Álvaro muttered. Watching her lilt toward the door, he thought of her in the ring with a vaquilla and all those idiot kids. His heart was racing. He turned to Ethan: "Don't take your eyes off her, not for a moment."

"I won't," Ethan said, nodding reflexively.

"A vaquilla is more dangerous than a *toro*." Seeing Ethan's puzzled expression, Álvaro explained his remark: "It's smaller and turns more quickly, so it's back on you faster. If the horn severs your femoral artery," he warned, pointing to his inner thigh, "they call for a priest to give you last rites."

"I understand you perfectly."

Ethan understood death and dying all too well, but Álvaro continued: "Don't encourage her to do something stupid."

"You know Rebeca—"

"Last rites," he repeated, his eyes burning into Ethan's as he backpedaled toward the wine racks. "I'm counting on *you*." He picked up a clipboard and began to take inventory.

"I'll do my best," Ethan said as his eyes fixed on Rebeca, who stood at an empty table by the front door, staring through the glass. Despite her stillness, he hurried after her, glancing outside as he did. The church's stone walls had a soft, reddish glow.

"Beautiful, isn't it?" Rebeca asked, undoing her ponytail.

"What's up with you? And what's with messing with the vaquilla?"

"Álvaro prefers my hair up," she said, "but this thing hurts my head." She stretched the scrunchy onto her wrist and slowly opened the door.

"He also prefers that you're in one piece."

"I was only kidding about the vaquilla, but I'd toss María Luisa into the ring if I could lift her fat ass."

"Don't start," Ethan chided and nudged Rebeca outside. "Your mom is looking forward to spending time with you. Don't ruin it."

Rebeca tousled her hair. "Sorry," she said with a wink and a look into La Rinconera. "I'll save my misbehaving for later."

17:05 h

Ethan's high school Spanish II class had included a one-week unit on bullfighting: lectures, still photos, vocabulary, a breeze of a written test, an oral presentation delivered without notes. Afterward, his interest piqued, Ethan had asked his *profesora* to borrow her copy of Larry Collins and Dominique Lapierre's *Or I'll Dress You in Morning*, a biography of the unorthodox matador Manuel Benítez, "El Cordobés," ("The Man from Córdoba"). She had gladly handed the paperback to him.

Ethan had devoured it three times, enthralled by bullfighting's pageantry and dance-like art. At graduation, his profesora had presented her copy of the book to him with a handwritten dedication. "So that you keep your love of bullfighting," it had read in Spanish. Grateful yet feeling guilty, he had bought her another copy at a used bookstore. He now owned the Spanish edition of the biography, too.

The arc of El Cordobés's life is riveting—dead-poor orphan, petty thief, construction worker, struggling novice, Spain's highest-paid matador, retired recluse. And told by expert storytellers, the moment-by-moment description of the rebel's debut in Madrid's famous Plaza de Toros de Las Ventas is a revelation in black and white. But in real life, a bullfight is gray and very red.

It had been during Ethan's exchange stay, watching the bloody ballet from the edge of his seat, when the bullfight had finally leapt off the page and into his face. The capework and the interplay had mesmerized him and taken his breath away. But as his in-person experiences had grown, so had his squeamishness during the spectacle, as brave bulls were put to the lance, dart, and sword. And when, after a fight, he had skimmed the pamphlet an anti-bullfighting protester had shoved at him, Ethan had been struck with the realization that he lacked consistency when it came to the treatment of animals. *How can the thought of my dog getting hurt or sick terrify me but the sight of a bull fighting fruitlessly for its life excite me?* he had asked himself.

While walking back to his host parents' piso, he had pondered the quote by Australian philosopher Peter Singer he had memorized for his oral presentation in Spanish II: "To protest about bullfighting in Spain . . . while continuing to eat eggs from hens who have spent their lives crammed into cages, or veal from calves who have been deprived of their mothers, their proper diet, and the freedom to lie down with their legs extended, is like denouncing apartheid in South Africa while asking your neighbors not to sell their houses to blacks."

By the time he had sunk into his "mattress" in his tiny bedroom, Ethan had felt confused and ashamed by his fascination with Spain's national blood sport. His shame and fascination had waxed and waned in the six years since then, adding to his confusion.

And now, a much more mature Ethan accepted that he could hold opposing opinions at the same time: Bullfighting was artful *and* cruel, and he was inconsistent *and* moral. His position on the future of the sport was straightforward: Let *el toro bravo* go the way of the dodo. But if Spanish pride and stubbornness refused to let it go, then eliminate the lance-wielding picador, and if the bull had to die, shoot it between the eyes.

He hadn't told his Spanish family that his love of going to the bulls had withered, and for that he wasn't proud of himself, as he usually wasn't. In Las Rozas's temporary bullring, Ethan sat quietly between María Luisa and Rebeca, not quite sure who was the rock and who was the hard place. At least they had good seats. In the small, third-category ring, everyone did.

Moments later, the bugle sounded, and a plumed *alguacilillo* in seventeenth-century clothing rode into the ring on a gray Andalusian. The stallion's long mane and tail bounced playfully as horse and rider high-stepped around the arena, clearing the ring. The duo jumped in place to the delight of the spectators and then loped harmoniously toward the bullfighters.

With their parade capes tied around them like slings, the three toreros and their cuadrillas waited just outside the inner ring, testing the sand. The lone picador remained out of sight.

"I really like that suit of lights," Sra. Navas said as the *paseíllo*, opening procession, began to the march of the pasodoble.

"Which one?" María Luisa asked.

"The tobacco and gold one."

"The gold's nice, but that shade of brown's not my thing."

"The fellow wearing it is quite handsome, though," Sra. Navas said.

María Luisa shook her head: "Not my thing either."

"Well, then, what *is* your thing?"

"I prefer blue, a grayish-blue."

Sra. Navas chuckled. "The banderillero? He's a little old for you, and a bit paunchy."

"Not a word," Ethan whispered to Rebeca as the parade passed.

She bit her tongue.

"I was talking about the color, not the old guy wearing it," María Luisa said.

The band fell silent as the paseíllo reached the *barrera*. Along the wooden wall the toreros and their subalternos traded their parade capes for magenta-and-yellow capotes and warmed up as the alguacilillo asked the president of the bullfight ("the mayor," Rebeca said) for the "keys" to the toril gate and delivered them to the *torilero*. The president waved his white handkerchief, the bugle blew, and the bullfighters took refuge behind the burladeros or in the alley-like *callejón* to prepare for the entrance of the bull. The torilero surveyed the ring and opened the toril. Pulses quickened. The spectators hushed.

You'll stay in there if you know what's good for you, Ethan told the bull in his mind.

The crowd waited.

Good boy.

And waited.

The torilero slapped the gate.

Don't go toward the light.

A chestnut bull with wide-set, upturned horns trotted into the ring.

Intelligent, but not quite enough, Ethan lamented as the athletic four-year-old began to explore. Two years ago, he had escaped the slaughterhouse when his aggression toward the horse had deemed him suitable for the bullfight, but because he was unsuitable for breeding, he was about to be slaughtered anyway. Ethan eyed his killer: *But that's the way it has to be, or he could quickly distinguish you from the cape.*

Wearing salmon pink, José María Martín was tall, gracefully slight of build, with long arms, and his eyes and those of the other members of his team were focused on the bull. What tendencies or quirks they saw in the animal now lingering in front of burladero number one Ethan did not know, but always the eager Spanish student, he felt slightly guilty about wanting to find out.

At the torero's request, a subalterno called the bull to burladero number two with a flash of magenta. The bull ran toward it and then stopped and stared at the subalterno. Separated from his herd and unable to find a way out of the ring, the animal's prized aggressiveness erupted. He scrabbled the sand mounded against the wooden shield, nodded twice, and butted the burladero repeatedly, violently, and instinctively. Ethan felt the thudding reverberations through his loafers.

"It favors its left horn," Rebeca noted.

"And?"

"Left-handed passes will be more dangerous," she explained as José María stepped out from behind his burladero. "They—"

"The torero," María Luisa interrupted, "carries the estoque in his right hand and doesn't use the sword to open the muleta during left-handed passes, or *naturales.*"

Holding the capote with both hands, José María called to the bull. It was the first time the animal had seen a man on foot inside an arena. He charged at a gallop and chased the cape through three series of fundamental yet skillful passes.

"The torero presents a smaller target by keeping the muleta closed," Rebeca said with a humph for her sister. "Better to wait until the torero changes capes to enlighten Ethan about those passes, don't you think?"

"He asked."

"Me, not you."

The bull's interest in the capote waned. Ignoring the torero's calls, he retreated to his *querencia*, favorite part of the ring, where he remained. The subalternos kept his attention.

"Thanks for the lesson," Ethan said with a pat on the shoulder for each of them.

María Luisa grinned. Rebeca shifted in her seat.

José María gestured toward the president, and, with a wave of the handkerchief, the wide door to the inner ring opened. The bugle sounded, the drum rolled, and the picador on a stocky, blindfolded horse wearing thick padding known as a *peto* plodded into the ring. The first *tercio*, third, had begun.

"I don't care for this part," Sra. Navas muttered as the picador positioned the horse's left flank against the barrera and waited for the bullfighters to draw the bull toward him. Responding to the movements of the capotes—fighting bulls are color blind—the bull edged closer to the horse and then charged, lifting and driving horse and rider into the barrier as the picador dug his lance into the mound of muscles above and behind the bull's neck, which shone with blood. "The poor horse."

José María teased the bull with his cape as the picador leaned vainly into his lance. Bloody yet instinctively determined, the bull refused to disengage. The spectators whistled their disapproval. "Butcher!" someone yelled as the picador continued to dig. The horse remained stoic; it would have been disemboweled as recently as the 1920s, before the introduction of the peto. Unlike Ernest Hemingway, Ethan would have found nothing comical about the helpless creature stepping on its own entrails.

"Damn, man," Sra. Navas mocked. "The poor thing."

Yelling and stomping the sand, José María lured the bull away, and he released. The subalternos scurried after him but were unable to keep him near the horse, and the animal trotted back to his querencia with his head held lower. The torero barked instructions to the picador and then followed him. The horseman's armored stirrups clanged against the peto as he repositioned himself in the saddle. He raised his lance and waited.

"The torero could waive the second *puyazo*," Rebeca whispered to Ethan, who began to stare at the bloody pike.

"I wish he would."

"But he won't," María Luisa said as José María aired the cape in front of the bull. The animal nodded twice. "He's still too dangerous."

Frowning, Rebeca leaned into Ethan. "I didn't say that he *would*, just that he *could*. He has that option in rings like this one."

Ethan watched the torero advance and retreat. The capework was enticing, drawing the bull toward the horse in fits and starts. A slave to animal instinct, the bull charged the horse as the picador dropped the tip of his lance like a pole vaulter approaching the box. Metal met muscle.

The picador dug, the horse staggered, the spectators booed.

Watching the bull thrust its left horn into the peto, Ethan was too busy feeling stupid to boo. *I never would have paid any attention.* He turned to Rebeca as the bullfighters overwhelmed the bull with their capotes, drawing it away from the horse and sending it back to his querencia. "It absolutely favors its left."

Rebeca smiled but said nothing. For a chatterbox, her silence spoke volumes.

Satisfied that some defect had been corrected or afraid that additional puyazos would spoil the bull, José María ordered the pricking to stop and, with a nod, asked for the change of tercio. The president waved his white handkerchief in agreement. The bugle blew.

"Only two?" Ethan asked.

"They rarely give three in Las Rozas," Rebeca said.

"And in Madrid?"

"Las Ventas is the most important bullring in the world," María Luisa volunteered. "There, he would have gotten another."

The picador trudged toward the wide door. It swung open.

Rebeca remained calm. "He still hooks a little. In Madrid, they would have tried to correct that tendency. There, *el público* is much more knowledgeable and demanding."

María Luisa turned to her mother. "Here in Las Rozas, the priority is finding husbands for unwed daughters, isn't that right, Mamá?"

"That subalterno wearing green has got a cute butt," Sra. Navas insisted.

"I'll pass."

The picador glanced again at the bull and then left the ring. The door closed, as did Ethan's least favorite stage of the bullfight; at least the final third's cruel steel was preceded by plastic intimacy and beautiful capework.

Alone in his querencia, the bull watched the men gather near the barrera. Something between a heart-stopping waste of time and a spurring necessity to further weaken the bull, the second tercio began.

Sra. Navas smiled. "This part I enjoy."

"Thrilling," Ethan agreed, watching José María limber up with two red-and-yellow banderillas in his hand. "I have a pair of those at home, real ones, except blue and yellow." The "little flags" were decorated with thick papers and had a metal barb at one end. He had bought the sticks years ago at a hole-in-the-wall that supplied toreros, along with a capote, a muleta, and the lighter, non-bladed sword the torero uses during most of the faena. They all hung in Ethan's home office. He had thought about taking them down, but it was easier to leave them where they were.

A one-time banderillero, José María had decided to place the first of three pairs himself. With his suit of lights sparkling like rosé champagne and his back arched ("cute butt," Sra. Navas said, elbowing María Luisa), he strutted as if in slow motion toward the bull and with an air that made Ethan envious. Ready to draw the bull away, a subalterno followed, another positioned himself to the left.

Reluctant to leave his querencia, the bull's glance shifted, settling on José María, who shuffled directly at him with his arms raised, inciting the animal. "¡Eh!" he yelled as the bull scrabbled the sand. He yelled again, lowering and raising the banderillas, bobbing his head, his black slippers sliding forward. The invasion provoked a charge. Man and bull met half way.

"The most exciting moment of the bullfight," Sra. Navas said.

José María faked right, zagged quickly left, and then launched himself with the barbs pointed heavenward. The bull charged past, thrusting his horns into what might have been as the banderillas were plunged into his hide. The chase was angry, vigorous, but short. The ovation was longer.

Uncomfortable, the bull swung his head from side to side. The wooden banderillas banged together and against his glistening flanks. The red paper grew redder.

The second pair followed.

And then the third.

More applause, more banging, another bugle blast, and the tercio closed.

Snotty and exhausted, the bull returned to his querencia under the watchful eyes of the subalternos as José María stood at the barrera with his back to his bloody dance partner. The torero draped his capote over the barrier, spoke briefly with a gentleman wearing a suit who Ethan surmised was the bullfighter's manager, and then took a few sips of water. He cracked his neck and traded the bottle for his *estoque simulado* and muleta.

My mouth would be dry, too, but my pants might not be, Ethan admitted to himself.

José María folded the cape over his arm, took the pommel of his sword in his left hand, crossed himself with his right, and started toward the president's box after a quick check of the bull that continued to guard his querencia.

Ethan watched the animal's attention shift from man to man. He carried his head less proudly, and his buoyancy would never return, but his fighting instinct was intact. And whether by offense or defense, luck or fate, he could easily even the score with the bony weapons on his head. The animal brain inside it knew nothing of right and wrong. He scrabbled the sand. *Fight bravely, obey the cape, keep your head down, and the público or the torero might ask that you be spared.*

Indultos were rarely granted.

But Ethan could hope. *You'd enjoy a life at stud.*

With his eyes focused on the bull he had just received permission to kill, José María opened the final third. He strode toward the center of the ring, removed his black velvet *montera*, and turned slowly around with the hat raised, dedicating the bull to the spectators, who applauded appreciatively. He tossed the montera over his shoulder.

"Bad luck," Rebeca said.

"It's considered bad luck for it to land upside down," María Luisa chimed in simultaneously.

Ethan nodded as the torero turned the hat over with the tip of his aluminum sword. The spectators' reactions were mildly mixed.

Holding the muleta's stick with his right hand and the estoque with his left, José María shook open the cape and broadened it with the sword. He hid the blade inside the heavy wool, tucked the hilt into his right palm, grasping both the stick and the hilt, and then tested his footing.

"I know what that stick is called," Ethan bragged to Rebeca. "Do you?"

"Which stick?"

"The dowel that's screwed into the muleta," he said.

"*Estaquillador*," María Luisa answered as the subalternos withdrew to the burladeros.

Rebeca shot forward. "Was he talking to you? I don't think so."

"I knew you didn't know the answer, although you should have."

"I know what I'd like to do with a tapered stick like that one," she snapped.

Ethan eased Rebeca back by the shoulder. "*Tranquila, guapa.*"

"I'm calm, I'm calm."

María Luisa shot her a look. "Ask me another," she told Ethan.

"Not right now," he said, exchanging a look with Sra. Navas. "Like being between a rock and a hard place, this seat," he joked halfheartedly.

"Take mine, if you'd like, my dear. I'm used to playing referee."

"They're grown women. I hope that won't be necessary."

"*¡Eh! ¡Eh!*" José María called. The bull nodded but did not charge.

"Let's just enjoy the show," Ethan said with another pat for each of Sra. Navas's daughters. *At least until the part*, he thought, *when that man plunges his sword between that bull's shoulder blades, probably misses the aorta and the heart, the animal dies gruesomely to smatters of applause, and they cut off one or both of his ears while he's still alive.*

"No problem here," María Luisa said.

The bull charged defensively as the torero invaded his querencia.

"Fine," Rebeca said with a broad smile. "See, he's started with right-handed passes."

"I do see that."

"*Derechazos*," María Luisa whispered almost politely.

Rebeca didn't bite. "Yes, thank you, María Luisa."

Like his suit, José María sparkled as he tantalized the bull. His style was orthodox and sedate. The pace of his cape was perfect, allowing the animal to attack the muleta without rushing the pass, as if the torero were in no obvious hurry for the horns to pass his body. Five times the bull chased the cloth, spun quickly, and returned without being called, and on the sixth a chest pass left him standing and panting. The bull's chestnut flanks glistened as the torero turned his back and swaggered away.

"I know what you're thinking, Mamá," María Luisa sighed: "nice ass."

"Am I wrong?" Sra. Navas asked with a wink. The old girl wasn't dead yet.

"No, but—"

"Well, if not that one, I know there's a cute butt out there for you." She caught Rebeca's attention as the torero inched toward the bull with the muleta in his left hand. "What do you think, *hija*?"

"My guy's already got a cute butt," her daughter said, "and I'm sure there's a cute butt out there for María Luisa, too . . . somewhere." She watched José María present the cape.

The bull nodded, as did Ethan, who began to pick at a splinter stuck in his sweater. His fingernails were much too short to do the job, and he regretted not renting a cushion.

The torero called the bull. More banging.

"Thanks, I think," María Luisa said, "but until your guy's got a ring on his finger, that cute butt isn't really yours."

"I know that."

"If you say so," María Luisa muttered. She took her eyes off the bull, which had finally responded to the torero's provocations, and took Ethan by the cuff. "You'd think these old bleachers would be worn smooth."

"You'd think so," he agreed, stomach growling.

Her long fingernails made quick yet careful work of the splinter. "Good to go."

"Thanks."

She reached for her purse. "I've got gum. It's limón, your favorite."

"Not right now," he said, distracted. He couldn't stand the thought of something happening to his favorite sweater. He pushed up his sleeves and returned most of his attention to the blood sport playing out in front of him.

Tiring and frustrated, the bull seemed less interested in José

María's fluid muleta than Ethan, who quietly—and wisely—named the passes to himself. Another growl of his stomach drowned in the rising crowd noise as the animal halted his charge in mid-natural and threw back his head. The left horn would have caught an unseasoned torero under the chin, but José María shuffled forward, pointed the sword at the cape, barking at the animal as he shook the cloth, and then enticed a finishing chest pass that left the bull stationary. The torero strutted back to the barrera.

Damn, Ethan lamented. He didn't need a watch to tell him the bull's twenty minutes were up. *It's the real sword for you, buddy.*

"Kill him, man," Rebeca said, tousling her hair. She moved her scrunchy to the other wrist. "You've gotten everything out of him."

Ethan watched the bullfighter trade swords. "*Matador*—Killer." The *estoque de muerte*'s steel blade shone in the lights as José María strode toward his condemned opponent. He paused near the bull's querencia, folded the cape over the sword again, and approached directly. He aired the broad muleta low and repeatedly in the bull's face and then backpedaled to draw him toward the center of the ring. There, farthest from rescue by the subalternos, the drama would play out. There, José María would demonstrate his valor with a difficult bull.

The deceit was irresistible.

The bull charged forward. And then again. A few meters short of dead center, he was coaxed into three short passes, and after a low flash of cloth he stood with his feet even and together. Ethan's heart pounded.

"Are you going to watch?" María Luisa asked.

"Are you?"

"You know it doesn't bother me."

Ethan had seen many bulls die, but nothing in his upbringing had conditioned him to handle death well. "Yes," he said. "I always do." No one back home understood how he could.

The moment of truth upon him, José María, the son of a meatpacker and a specialist in *la suerte de matar*, the act of killing, stood in front of the bull's right horn. Except for his labored breath, the animal stood stock still with his head down and his eyes focused on the cloth held low before him. The torero raised his right hand, placed the pommel of the estoque de muerte against his chest, and took aim, sighting down the slightly curved blade between the horns and at his target: the withers.

Ethan rocked backward. The translations of "running sword thrust" and "receiving" flashed into his mind as the torero raised the sword to chest height and extended it. *Must be "recibiendo."*

José María twitched the muleta as he called to the bull.

No pricks. No bone. A clean death.

The bull charged . . .

Of the six sword thrusts that afternoon, two were perfect. Ethan felt privileged to have seen them. And by bullfighting standards, four of the six deaths were clean.

But as the mule teams dragged the corpses out of the arena, Ethan felt nothing but dirty.

19:15 h

Sra. Navas's favorite place to sit in La Rinconera was at the bar, on the stool closest to the register. Worrying over the drawer was where her husband spent most of his time, and she loved to be near him. Alcohol, however, held nothing for her, save an occasional glass of a light-bodied Tempranillo with tapas. This evening, her seat was occupied, as were all the spots at the bar, but she didn't mind crowding around a table with her kids.

Her arthritic knees were predicting rain, but Álvaro had insisted there was no medical support for a connection between health and weather: "It's the walk to and from the bullring." She hadn't entirely dismissed her future son-in-law's comment, but there are certain things a person just knows. And a mother's intuition is often spot on. Seated in a comfortable chair borrowed from "El Acueducto," Sra. Navas spat out the olive pit she'd been sucking on and picked up a bit of bread. "It's sure to be chilly at the concert."

María Luisa's mouth was full of roasted peppers. She hummed her agreement.

"Do your old mother a favor and dress warmly, or take a blanket."

"I'm going to put on layers," Ethan said and spooned another bite of *ensalada rusa*, Spanish potato salad of Russian origin made with peas, tuna, diced eggs, and heavy mayonnaise. Rebeca had barely touched hers; she had that look on her face again. He gave her a nudge. "Look, guapa, no hot sauce."

"I've fallen on my back and can't get up," she laughed softly, using the idiom she had taught him years ago. "What, did you forget to bring it with you?"

Álvaro approached the table. "Forget to bring what with him?"

"His bottle of hot sauce," María Luisa said. "Mamá's recipe doesn't need it, unlike that insipid stuff we had the other day at the BurgoCentro."

Chewing, Ethan nodded.

"We only serve the best," Álvaro agreed with a wink for Sra. Navas and then a kiss on the top of the head for Rebeca. She wasn't wearing her scrunchy. "Can I bring you all anything? Ethan, how about another Fanta Limón?"

"I'm good, thanks."

"A *café cortado*, please," Sra. Navas said. One of the few things she enjoyed more than being waited on was nursing a good cup of coffee.

"Anyone else?"

Rebeca tousled her hair. "I think we're fine."

"Back in a moment, then."

Rebeca shook her empty can of Fanta Orange: "Any more, and I'll have to pee during the concert."

"Amén," María Luisa said in rare agreement with her sister. She forked a bite of roasted pepper and offered it to Ethan.

"No thanks," he said.

"They're really good."

"I'm sure, but so is this *ensalada*."

María Luisa scraped off the charred bits with her knife. "What about now?" she asked, pointing the fork at him.

"Insistent, aren't you?"

She shrugged her shoulders. "We are what we are. So . . . last chance. You can't get peppers like these—"

"Leave the boy alone, María Luisa," Sra. Navas said.

"Yes, leave him alone," Rebeca agreed. "He doesn't want your germs. Nobody wants your germs."

María Luisa shot her a look and then angrily ate the bite herself.

As she did, Álvaro returned with a white cup and saucer and two pots balanced on a server's tray. He poured the strong espresso, stained it with two drops of scalded milk, and placed the cup, a spoon, and one tubular sugar packet in front of Sra. Navas. She wasn't a picky woman, but he knew how she preferred things.

"Thank you, my dear."

"Anything else?"

"We're fine," Rebeca repeated. Four sides of white were showing in each of her eyes.

Álvaro rubbed Rebeca's shoulder, his eyes trailing down her back. "I'll check back later, then," he said with a polite yet frustrated smile and left. She was wearing that pair of jeans with the hearts on the pockets. On the shoulder wasn't where he wanted to touch her.

"We should have asked him about the electrician," Rebeca said. "I'm curious to find out how much we have to tighten our belts."

"Better to ask Papá about it," Sra. Navas said; "I'll talk to him later."

Rebeca spooned a bit of ensalada rusa. "*You* could stand a smaller belt anyway," she told María Luisa.

"And *you* could stand a bigger bra, but I guess you're going to have to get pregnant to finally get boobs."

"There's nothing wrong with my boobs," Rebeca huffed almost to herself.

"That's enough, girls."

"What's wrong with my boobs?" she asked.

María Luisa stretched phonily, arching her back. "They're nothing out of this world."

"Girls, I said that's enough."

"But they're perfect."

"Hardly," María Luisa snorted.

"I won't tell you again."

"Let's get a man's opinion," Rebeca said. "Ethan, is there anything wrong with my boobs? Be honest."

"Rebeca, that's quite enough," Sra. Navas chided before Ethan, who sat flustered, could fumble an answer.

20:00 h

Ethan didn't deny that God might exist, but he believed that most adherents to organized religion were frauds, six-days-a-week sinners, ignorants, or merely creatures of habit. Hard scientists didn't have all the answers either, but if a divine being were manipulating the strings of reality, the invisibility and scope of those strings ran counter to Ethan's logical side. Science and faith had always been at odds; religions, too. Interfaith families were often full of religious strife, yet intrafaith families weren't exempt from the discord.

Ethan was the product of a mixed Christian marriage: Roman Catholic bride, Protestant groom. The tension had begun during the engagement—pre-cana (priest-led, premarital counseling) and signatures on an agreement that the children would be raised Catholic. *It's the Catholic way or no way*, Ethan's father had realized, but in hindsight his concessions had neither prevented conflict nor fostered religiousness in his son.

Maybe if the gymnasium-of-a-church back home had looked and felt like the one Rebeca stared at from her balcony, Ethan might have stomached that last year of Confraternity of Christian Doctrine classes, been confirmed, and made Mom and Grandma proud. If the closing of a brainwashed circle could even engender meaningful pride.

Sra. Navas had never given much thought to Ethan's faith. He was a good boy when she met him, and he had grown into a good man, imperfectly perfect in ways she accepted but kept wisely to herself. He had gone to church with her once or twice, but she had never seen him reading the Bible.

None of her kids attended mass as religiously as she did or spent hours alone with the Word of God. Nevertheless, she had no doubt they all had a strong sense of right and wrong. That sense in Ethan was unwavering, but as she sat in her bedroom, she prayed he could find the courage to stray. For her sake.

In the front of the apartment, Ethan, María Luisa, and Rebeca lounged in the salón.

The room was an unpretentious, plastered rectangle furnished for comfort in earth tones with splashes of color, including a green and pinkish-purple centerpiece that reminded Ethan of the fireweed he and his mother had seen in Alaska the year before she died.

Two bookcases held family photos, Sra. Navas's collection of terra-cotta figurines, and an accumulation of books, including Spanish classics, all of which Ethan had read, and a set of encyclopedias that languished on the shelf for months at a time.

Near the couch, the apartment's only television set was off. Its screen reflected the silhouette of Rebeca in her favorite chair by the balcony. The doors were open, but the sheer curtains hung lifelessly except for fitful flutters caused by Rebeca's gesticulations with the October edition of *AplausoS*. She had gotten bored with the bullfighting magazine on page two, but Spaniards talk with their hands, and the rolled-up monthly was a helpful prop.

"Enough about that," Rebeca said. "I'm famished."

María Luisa poked at the couch. "I'm not surprised."

"I'm not surprised either," Ethan said. "You just picked at your food."

"I didn't feel like eating."

"Any particular reason?"

"She's pregnant," María Luisa laughed. "I'm joking, of course. I'd have to be."

"Don't go there."

"Ask Álvaro."

"Shut your fat mouth."

Ethan tucked his hands underneath him and turned to the busybody beside him. "What's with your . . . fascination?"

"More like obsession," Rebeca growled.

María Luisa smiled. "Virgins have a hard look, and judging by her mood lately, maybe something hard would soften her up." She poked again at the couch. "And I know how much a grandchild would mean to our parents."

Rebeca nearly threw the magazine at her. "Nothing will ever replace the loss of Félix."

"I know that."

"Do you?"

"Your and Álvaro's child will be a blessing. This apartment needs more joy."

"I won't be living in this piso for much longer."

"Thank God," María Luisa mumbled. "But you'll visit."

"You want me to visit?"

"Visits are fine. Besides, babies are fun."

"*You* have one, then. If you can ever get a date."

"I'm working on it."

The words raised Rebeca's hackles. "That's news to me. And from what I hear, you'll be moving out soon, too. Your leaving *alone* will bring more joy to this apartment."

"Wanting me out and getting me out are two different things," María Luisa said snottily.

"Perhaps, but your days are numbered."

Ethan tore his eyes off his wrist—no watch. "I bet the minutes before the concert are numbered, too."

"We've got time," María Luisa said and tried to reengage her sister. "Worry about—"

"I'm not so sure. We have to eat first. Rebeca needs to eat."

"Rebeca needs to—"

Ethan shook his head. "None of this is helping."

"I think she needs to hear it."

"*None* of this is your concern either," Rebeca shouted.

As a child of divorce, Ethan had a high tolerance for discomfort, but his seat on the couch didn't feel as comfortable anymore. He stood up, shoved his hands in his pockets, and pointed with his chin toward the balcony. "I bet the neighbors are getting quite an earful."

Rebeca slammed the magazine against the chair. "I really don't care."

"Well, I do, young lady," Sra. Navas barked, barging into the salón. "I could hear the two of you from my bedroom. Whatever is going on, stop it. Now."

"Sorry, Mamá," Rebeca whimpered.

María Luisa wasn't so quick with her apology, but stood up. "Ethan, *vámonos.*"

"And where do you think you're going?" Sra. Navas asked, sliding in front of her.

"We need to get something to eat, and I need a break from *her* before the concert."

"I'll go," Rebeca volunteered.

"Then go," María Luisa said with a smile.

Sra. Navas glanced at Ethan, who shrugged his shoulders. "No one is going anywhere until I find out what's going on."

No one said a word.

"I'm waiting."

"This isn't my fight," Ethan begged, "and I'd really rather not get involved." He retreated toward the dining table and sat down to wait it out.

"Of course, my dear," Sra. Navas said and turned back to María Luisa. "Well?"

"It's not my fault she's a prude."

"Oh, shut the hell up," Rebeca snapped.

"Quiet, both of you."

Ethan continued to stare at where his watch would have been.

María Luisa glanced toward the front door. "I apologize for my tone, but that's all. We need to go. Ethan, ready?"

"Sit down."

"I said I'd go," Rebeca humphed, jumping up.

"Both of you sit down." Sra. Navas sighed heavily as they obeyed, and then exchanged a look with Ethan. "Time to play referee. My dear, go get yourself a snack while I speak to these two. There's a new package of fairy cakes and a bottle of Limón. Eat in my room and shut the door. I'll make dinner when I'm done, *vale?*"

Happy to oblige, he nodded and shuffled out, but the women were at it again before he opened the refrigerator door. He hurried as best he could.

"Rebeca's relationship isn't your concern," Sra. Navas declared as she shut the balcony doors.

"She would do well to listen to what I have to say—"

"I have no *puñetero* interest in what you have to say."

Puñetero meant "damned." It and countless slang terms had leapt off the mile-a-minute tongues of Ethan's classmates at El Instituto. Using slang expressions had helped Ethan fit in with the group, but Rebeca had generally taught him words and phrases with a broader use. He ran through them as he nudged the door closed, and then sat down on the bed to eat. He chewed loudly, drowning out the world.

"Your fiancé was interested in what I have to say," María Luisa continued.

Sra. Navas became as short and frosted as her hair. "Shut it, hija."

"Álvaro was just being polite," Rebeca fibbed, running her fingers through her hair. "I know about your conversation . . . and your advice."

Sra. Navas's eyes widened. "Your advice?"

Neither daughter chose to elaborate.

"Did you give Álvaro advice?" Sra. Navas asked, arms akimbo.

María Luisa nodded.

"And just *what* did you say?"

Silence.

"Well?"

María Luisa's back stiffened. "Álvaro's frustrated . . . sexually."

"And?"

"And . . ."

"Oh, just say it," Rebeca sneered. "Why shut your fat face now?"

"Mamá already knows. She just wants to make me say the words."

"So say them."

"Fine."

"We're waiting—"

"Rebeca won't pleasure her man, in any way."

Sra. Navas crossed herself as the words passed her daughter's lips.

"The poor guy's wearing out his hand in the bathroom because she's a cock tease or frigid. I'm not sure which one's worse."

"I'm neither one, you heifer."

"I might be fat, but I'm not the one who makes my fiancé jerk off, lord knows."

"*Might* be fat?"

"Girls, that's enough—"

"And you don't even have a man, let alone a fiancé."

"I said I'm working on it, and the man I love, the man I truly know I'm supposed to be with, will *never* have to substitute his hand for mine."

The hairs on the back of Sra. Navas's neck stood on end, but she remained oddly quiet. The girls were too busy sparring to notice.

"Men jerk off all the time," Rebeca barked. "It's just what they do. Álvaro's no different; he'd masturbate regardless."

"Absolutely right," María Luisa conceded. The point of agreement brought a curious smile to Sra. Navas's worried face. "But I'm not telling you to whore yourself around town, servicing every guy who gets an erection. You're not going to go to hell for letting the man you truly love make love to you, whether you're married or not."

"Yeah, right," Rebeca scoffed, but the words contradicted her subtle change in expression.

"But if you really love him, and he really loves you, it's not a sin either."

Sra. Navas crossed herself again.

"Where did you hear that?"

"Somewhere," María Luisa said. "The point is, you won't go to hell for pleasuring your future husband, but you might condemn yourself to a lifetime of regrets if you push him away."

Rebeca opened her mouth but sat back instead. Except for the rattle of the taberna below, silence came over the salón, as if the three women were lost in the unexpected echoes of a perfectly struck note.

Moments later María Luisa rose. "May I go?" she asked without a hint of her previous tone. "Poor Ethan's going to think he's back living with that awful host family if he has to stay in that room."

"Yes," Sra. Navas said. "What about dinner?"

"We'll fend for ourselves," María Luisa answered and then hurried out of the room.

"Don't be late for the concert. And take a coat."

"I'll meet you there," Rebeca shouted.

Moments later Ethan thumped down the hall and into his bedroom, shutting the door.

"He's angry."

"I don't think so."

He soon reappeared wearing a curious expression and a shirt under his sweater. "See you later," he whispered with a wave as he passed the salón. He knocked on María Luisa's door, and the two of them left the apartment, their voices fading as they descended the flight of stairs.

"He's probably shell shocked from all the yelling," Rebeca said. "Why won't she mind her own business?"

The question drew no response.

"Mamá?"

"Sí, hija."

"I said I was wondering why María Luisa won't keep her nose out of my business. She drives me crazy."

Sra. Navas's gaze remained fixed on the bookcase. "I know. Don't I know, but try to focus on the message, not the messenger."

Rebeca was caught between surprise and expectation. She became unusually pensive and said nothing for what to her seemed an eternity. "I can't be hearing you correctly."

"You're a beautiful and intelligent woman," her mother said proudly.

"What I'm hearing you say is . . . have sex." Rebeca tilted her head. "That can't be what my mother is saying."

"I'm not."

"Then what are you saying?"

"Only you know if Álvaro is the right one. *The* one, the one about which you are as certain as this uncertain world will let you be."

"And?" Rebeca asked, dropping the magazine on the floor.

"And if he isn't, keep looking for the one who is."

"And if I've already found him?"

"Then do what that inner voice"—Sra. Navas gestured toward the church—"'they' say comes from God is telling you."

"What if I don't have one?" Rebeca asked quizzically.

"You do."

"I'm not sure I can trust it."

"You can if you're being honest with yourself."

"You're the second person to give me that advice."

Sra. Navas frowned. "If the first was Álvaro—"

"He wasn't," Rebeca said, staring into her mother's eyes, which were clouded, but her judgment was clear. "What should I do, Mamá?" she asked almost helplessly.

"Only you can know."

"What would *you* do?"

"I can't make the decision for you."

"I know, but if you could . . ."

Sra. Navas cleared her throat. "You have to make your own decisions, and I have to let you make them. I don't and won't always agree with what you decide, but I'm not meant to. All I ask is that you are safe and that you choose to be happy. Don't be afraid to be happy."

Rebeca grinned. "I made that decision this afternoon."

"I won't ask, but I hope you've thought it through."

"I've never given anything so much thought."

"That's my girl." Sra. Navas's wistful wrinkles softened as they hugged. "Just be safe."

"I will. We will."

Sra. Navas's mind swam with emotion. "Take the journey together, come what may."

21:15 h

Thomas had kept a low profile since his brush with the old man. No one but Marisa had missed him. Holed up in the playhouse on the church grounds, he took another swig of Coke, set the can back on its sweaty ring, and rotated it until the Coke ribbon faced him. The floor was littered with natural debris and pipas hulls, but he resisted the urge to start cleaning.

Anxiety-provoking thoughts of the days ahead flashed through his mind. Not one for inflicting pain, unlike the bracelet-selling bully at the Plaza de España, he still hadn't found an "acceptable" way to delay the return home. *But that thug got exactly what he wanted.*

Teetering between desperation and resignation, he wondered what it would take to tip things in the wrong—or was it the right?—direction. He tugged four times at the bracelet around his wrist, tucked the leather out of sight—

A little more.

He turned the Coke can a millimeter and then eased his hand toward the zipper on his chest—

Too far.

He "fixed" the can and reached again for the zipper. He slid it up a centimeter—

Another hair.

He "refixed" the can and slid the zipper down two centimeters—

Nope.

He "re-refixed" the can and reached for the zipper—

98

He grabbed the can, took a swig, set the can back on its sweaty ring, and rotated it until the Coke ribbon faced him. The aluminum stuck to his fingertips, and the can quivered in place.

Not if my life depended on it. A little more. Last time, I promise.

Helplessness, self-loathing, suffering . . .

"What are you doing in here?" a familiar voice interrupted.

"Taking refuge," Thomas said.

"Why here?"

"This spot is better."

They often retreated to the playhouse for conversations that were anything but childish. "Better for what?" Marisa asked with a grin that was plain to see. Her mind and her mouth had been busy, but she still hadn't gotten the taste of him she wanted.

"Wipe that smile off your face," he reproved her with a chuckle, but he had to admit that under very different circumstances he would have opted for release. Lina, however, was the one he wanted. He hadn't the slightest doubt. The torch he carried for her burned as bright as concentrated sunlight, even though her focus remained elsewhere and he could never stand up to scrutiny under her father's magnifying glass. "The zipper on my chest is the only thing going down."

"I just want to talk," Marisa fibbed and plopped down beside him. The scent of perfume. "But I'm not apologizing for being in love with you."

"I'm not asking you to," he said without looking at her.

"And I'm not apologizing for the other thing either."

"I'm not asking you to," he repeated.

"Besides, you can't blame a girl for trying, can you?"

"I guess not," he said with a shrug, still staring at the can.

She wiggled closer and reached across him. Her jacket fell open, exposing a T-shirt with a deep V-neck.

"*¡Oye!* Hands to yourself."

"Get your mind out of the gutter," she said, her arms hovering above his thighs. "I just want a sip of Coke."

"Fine," he said, doubting her.

She gulped down the can and hid it behind her.

"Just a sip, huh?"

She fumbled with her jacket, opening it even more. "You can't blame a girl for being thirsty," she said with a wink.

"You really are incorrigible."

"I know, but that's what you love about me."

Her words hung on the dusky air, and the two sat in awkward silence, listening to a cricket serenade.

She pressed her luck when the insect fell quiet. "Did you know Mercedes didn't marry for love?"

The change of topic caught him off guard, but he welcomed it. "I—I know she loved her husband."

"Not at first. They didn't consummate the marriage for some time."

"Poor guy."

"She married to escape the war."

"I've had enough talk about the war today," Thomas said and reached for his wrist.

Marisa nodded, remembering what he had told her about the old fascist at the church. She eased Thomas's hand back onto the floor. "Don't worry about that."

"I'm not worried that, about that."

"That old man's an asshole. Screw him." What *she* wanted to screw was right beside her. "Anyway, Mercedes did what she had to."

"She must have loved him eventually. They had a child."

"She did. And they did, God rest his soul, but Mercedes says the sex never became making love."

Thomas took his eyes off Marisa. "Sad," he said, reaching for a withered leaf. Fall would soon fade into winter, which would melt into spring. Thomas hated that change of season. As winter's merciful darkness gave way to cruel sunlight, his brain would tilt longer and longer at windmills. Earlier and earlier, the depressing dawn would stick its fingers in his eyes, highlighting each troublesome speck and bit and stain. Mental exhaustion would set in before the real work had even begun. Night would fall later and later, and then be gone in the blink of a snoozy eye or the flick of an obsessively and compulsively cleaned switch.

"They made a good life together, and for that and for Churro she's thankful."

"We're all thankful for Churro," Thomas said, silhouetting the broad leaf against the window. He thought of the maple tree back home. And syrup. And pancakes and bacon; how he missed the sweet and salty pleasure of syrup-covered bacon. "And I'm thankful for the home cooking these past weeks. I don't get a lot of that."

"You don't get *any* of that," Marisa said. "How long has it been since you cooked or baked anything at home?"

"Years."

"That's hard to imagine."

"Not when you've got this damn brain."

"What about the microwave?"

"The microwave is as dusty as the stove," he said. "I just reset their clocks. Fucking power outages."

"How long does that take?"

"Sometimes the clocks blink for hours, sometimes for days," he said matter-of-factly, "until I get the courage to touch them." And when he did, he did so with the corner of a fingertip he had wiped off seventeen, twenty-seven, or thirty-seven times, depending on the moment. The world wouldn't end if he left a fingerprint, just his world.

Marisa's overactive mind changed gears. "I would cook for you if—"

"We . . . I don't use the kitchen."

"You told me you use the refrigerator."

Thomas's mind wandered to that damn appliance. He had ground the black off the rubber handles with the bottom of countless T-shirts. The chrome was covered with a fine powder, the color of which matched the color of the shirts. He tended to leave the grindings because once he started blowing them off, he couldn't stop. "I use it occasionally."

"But you *do* use it."

"For milk, if there's cereal, but that's rare. Yogurt, cold cuts, leftover pizza (*thank God for delivery pizza*), and weight-loss shakes." Those vitamin-packed meals in a can were a godsend. "The freezer not so much." On good days he tried popsicles or ice cream sandwiches—sandwiches, never quarts. He would meticulously tear the top flaps off the box, place it in the freezer door, and then arrange the treats inside the box. Easing the door closed was essential to keep the popsicles or sandwiches from shifting.

"That's a start," Marisa hoped, but she really had no intention of trying to change him. "I do worry about your diet. Preservatives aren't good for you."

Untoasted Pop-Tarts, pouches of tuna (cans had to be drained), granola bars, packages of crackers, plain peanut butter sandwiches (jams and jellies were perishable luxuries to live without), and twelve-packs of store-brand water and soft drinks were affordable and easy to manage.

They were kept, along with napkins, foam plates, plastic dinnerware, and shopping bags that had passed his inspection, in a large box next to the recliner. What didn't fit inside the box he neatly stacked on top of it or on the floor beside it. "I know, but I don't want to talk about food. I hate food. The rigmarole of containers and lids, bottles and caps, except for—"

She could have completed the sentence for him, but he didn't have to tell her twice. "How about a story, then?"

"Does it involve food?"

"Yes, but it's not *about* food."

Thomas set the leaf on the floor and spun it until the stem pointed at Marisa. "Is it about sex?" He knew her too well.

Marisa smiled. "It's about a couple, while they were dating."

"Do I know this couple?"

"Stop asking so many questions," she said, still smiling.

"It's about sex."

"Quiet. Do you want to hear it or not?"

It's about sex, Thomas told himself, but he nodded.

"*Bien*, so near Valladolid there's a little town called Portillo that's famous for its garlic, and it holds a festival that celebrates it: the *Feria del Ajo*, as you could probably guess. Some years ago, a young man who was—*is* a nut for garlic and his girlfriend had spent the day at the *feria* and were driving home in an old SEAT that belonged to his father."

"Sociedad Española de Automóviles de Turismo," Thomas volunteered.

She smacked him on the knee. "Don't interrupt. Well, the car was reliable but the gas gauge wasn't, and they began to run out about an hour from home. No big deal since there was a full can in the trunk."

"Good thinking."

"They pulled over, he got out, grabbed the can, and as he was poking around for a funnel, it started to rain. Not hard, just a drizzle. And the light in the trunk didn't work either."

"Sounds like quite a car," Thomas laughed as his mind wandered. He pictured the aging, five-speed parked at the airport back in the States. The red Honda's dull finish, abused fuel tank door, and peeling trim belied his love for that car—another victim of his disorder.

"SEATs have gotten better over the years."

"I hope so."

"Anyway, she heard him poking around, and before he could ask her to get the flashlight out of the glove compartment, she was standing beside him, shining a light on everything but a funnel."

"Where was the funnel?"

"Hell if I know, and the can didn't have one of those reversible spouts either. Eventually, they gave up, but not before the light was just about dead."

"Spare batteries?"

"Not even one. She just kept tapping on the flashlight."

"And praying," he added with a wry smile.

"So as he was struggling to put gas in the tank, the skies opened up, and the rain started to bucket down. He spilled gas on himself, they were soaked, and even though it was June she got cold . . . and her nipples—"

"Her summer dress wasn't leaving much to the imagination. I get your drift."

"She was a looker in her day, but the smell of gasoline made her nauseated and gave her a terrible headache."

"And off went his pants, right? Here comes the sex."

Marisa slapped his knee again. "Keep interrupting, and I'm going to give your lips something else to do."

He wagged his finger at her.

"Anyhow, he told her to get back in the car and wrap up in the picnic blanket. She did, and a few moments later she heard him slam the trunk. He got in, cranked the car, turned up the heat, and the two of them had a laugh shivering there on the side of the road."

"What about the pants?"

"They were in the trunk."

"Off went his pants," Thomas smirked. "I told you."

"Not so fast, smartass. His father painted houses for a living, and he kept a change of clothes in the trunk. He just put on his father's pants. They were enormous, and *they* were wearing *him*, but he wasn't half naked."

"When did they have sex, then?"

Marisa grinned. "He just drove her home."

"It must have been after."

"He walked her to the door, gave her a sweet kiss, went home, and the next day bought himself a new funnel. She was dry and in bed before her parents got home from church."

"And?"

"And about a month later, he asked her father for his blessing. When they had saved enough money, they got married, bought a piso, had kids." Her words trailed off as she watched Thomas reach for his wrist but stop himself. She inched closer. "Life's been no fairy tale, but they're still together."

"Fairy tales don't exist," he mumbled, but even so, Lina was his princess. Not the bullshit Disney beauty, but a flawed yet warmhearted cutie with full cheeks and a gravelly laugh who had been under his skin long before he walked in on her that morning. The intrusion had been completely accidental, but he had deliberately kept the memory alive—her moss green bra and panties lying on the bed, her wet hair, the bounce of surprise of her tear-drop breasts, her narrow waist. He could still see the towel falling.

But Lina wasn't waiting for her prince, and even if she were, there was nothing charming about obsessive-compulsive disorder. Thomas shook his head. "What's the point of this story?"

"You're horny."

"The point of a story about an old couple who I may or may not know is that I'm horny?"

"Precisely, judging by the number of times you've mentioned sex. I never said a word about sex."

"With you, I just assumed."

"Never assume," Marisa said playfully, wagging her finger at him. "But there's a second point that goes hand in hand with the first."

"Which is?"

"You haven't spoken that bitch's name."

Bitch was one of her milder insults, and he let it pass. "Lina's always on my mind."

"Not once," she smirked, "*and* I've made you feel better."

Thomas glanced out the window. The bell tower was bathed in soft light. Behind it, a handful of stars peeked here and there through a thin layer of clouds. For all that Marisa had done for him, she deserved as many thanks as there were bodies in the heavens, but he managed to say only one: "Thank you."

"There's a third point, too," Marisa said without the slightest care for the world outside.

"You're good," he said, impressed. "I'm all ears."

Quivering, she took him by both hands. "Improbable events *can* lead to a happy ending," she whispered, placing his palms on her excited breasts and squeezing.

22:30 h

The door Ethan was holding was made of *ajenjo*, wormwood. He had just learned that word from Rebeca. She had learned it from her father when she was little, when she used to proudly hold the door for him as he flipped through the mail. Ethan would make it today's word of the day. Yesterday's word was "*otorrinolaringólogo*—ear, nose, and throat specialist." Quite a mouthful. The day before yesterday's word was "*antepenúltimo*—third from last." Ethan enjoyed learning obscure words like that.

"Let's go," Rebeca said. She shut and locked the family's mailbox and sprang out of the vestibule. "We're not waiting for María Luisa."

Ethan agreed with a halfhearted nod and followed her. They exchanged pleasantries with a neighbor exiting La Rinconera and then began the short walk down Avenida de la Constitución to the Plaza Mayor. "Where *is* your sister?"

"Apparently, she's out."

"Out where?"

"I don't ask, and I don't care," Rebeca said, already a few steps ahead of him.

"I guess she'll meet us at the concert, then."

"Stop worrying about my sister." She took Ethan by the sleeve and pulled him toward the corner. The side street was packed with cars as far as they could see. Silhouettes chatted and smoked outside Taberna de Regiones. "She's a big girl. A really big girl—"

"Be nice," Ethan said.

"I just meant she can take care of herself." With a burst of energy and a laugh, she towed him across the street and looked for a way to get onto the sidewalk.

"Liar, liar, pants on fire," he said, being tugged past two kissing subcompacts and an illegally parked motorcycle.

Rebeca released him and squeezed between a Smart car and a *furgoneta*, small van: a word of the day from years ago.

Ethan marveled at how lithely she moved. *Those back pockets are literally the seat of Álvaro's sexual frustration*, he chuckled, staring at her. *Imagine that.* He thumped after her.

"Tight fit," she said. "Really tight for a 'big girl.' You know, one who's swollen with pride at how well she can handle herself."

"You're such a liar," he laughed, brushing imaginary dirt off his khakis: a ruse to fiddle with the socks tied below each knee.

Rebeca patted herself and then gestured toward the standpipe built into the building next to them. "Yeah, these jeans are on fire. You better hose me down."

"Tempting, but no. You're going to be cold enough."

"Why's that?"

"You didn't listen to your mother. No coat, no blanket," Ethan said.

"This turtleneck is really warm. Besides, I make my own decisions."

"Now who's the 'big girl'?"

"Keep it up and you'll be the one who gets hosed down," Rebeca said with a playful elbow as she glanced into La Rinconera. "El Acueducto" was full. "By me, of course, not María Luisa."

"Why would she hose me down?"

"Don't worry, my sister wouldn't know what to do with a 'hose' if her lonely life depended on it."

Ethan could barely contain himself. "You're going to hell for that one."

"Not for that one," she said, watching Álvaro wait on a table. "Not for any one, I hope."

"Am I supposed to know what that means?"

"Not yet," Rebeca sighed, but the dip in her mood was as brief as the flick of her hair. "*Vámonos.*" She lilted past the spot where the salty-mouthed neighbor had been blocked in by the movers, smiled at a passing couple, and was soon two steps ahead of him.

Recalling her "tears of joy" on the balcony that afternoon, Ethan's mind and feet began to race: *Maybe Álvaro's frustration is about to come to an end.* He acknowledged the couple without slowing. "What's the hurry, guapa?"

"No hurry."

Ethan stared at her jeans: no smoke, no flames. But he had his doubts. "I don't believe you."

"Why not?"

"Because Spaniards don't do anything quickly."

She walked backward. "*¡Jaaa-jaaa!*"

"Except for speaking, of course. And some of you just can't shut up."

"Keep it up, funnyman, and you won't get your surprise."

"My surprise?"

Near the intersection, a woman wearing a vendor tray stepped out of the crowd. After calling to Rebeca, she pulled the neck strap over her head and set the tray on the sidewalk.

"Someone wants you," Ethan told Rebeca, pointing at the woman.

Rebeca glanced over her shoulder. "That's your surprise," she said, turning around, and then glided away from him. When she reached the woman, Rebeca took an exaggerated step over the neck strap, and she and the woman cheek kissed hello.

As Ethan approached them, the two were laughing about their brief stints in mountain guide school. Apparently, the only thing Rebeca had been good at was getting tangled in the climbing ropes.

"I'd like you to meet an old friend," Rebeca told the woman, taking Ethan by the sleeve again. There was something sweet about his bashfulness when it came to meeting females for the first time. "Paloma, this is Ethan. Ethan, Paloma."

"*Encantada*—Pleased to meet you," the woman said and stepped toward him.

He slid forward. "*Encantado.*"

They brushed cheeks and made kissing sounds.

High school Spanish had prepared Ethan for many of the things he had experienced during his exchange stay, but cheek kissing wasn't one of them. His first time had been awkward and confusing, and, for a boy who had never gotten close to a girl during high school, he had had a tingle of excitement. In Spain, the greeting was nonsexual and common, and kissing the right cheek first may have been one of Ethan's more important lessons as an exchange student.

Ethan and Paloma separated. He was hardly blushing.

"Paloma has something for you," Rebeca told Ethan.

"Is that so?"

Paloma reached into her tray and pulled out a tube of dark-colored pipas. "Rebeca's being modest. These were her idea; I'm just the one who made them."

"Thank you very much," he stuttered, taking the sunflower seeds, which upon closer inspection were a familiar shade of red.

Paloma reached back into her tray and handed him his hot sauce. "And it was her idea to 'borrow' this, so if you've missed it, blame her."

"You're a liar *and* a thief," Ethan joked. He squeezed the familiar bottle that he would have sworn was still in the kitchen. "For how long?" he asked Rebeca as he hugged her. She was cold.

"Long enough. And good thing Papá's ensalada rusa didn't need hot sauce."

Ethan was still grinning. "Tricky, tricky."

"Your first going-away present," Rebeca said.

"Thank you both. I'll enjoy them soon."

Paloma picked up her tray. "You're very welcome."

"How much do I owe you?" Ethan asked.

"Nothing, Rebeca's already taken care of it. And if I don't get back to work, it will be my only sale." She turned to go. "Are you two staying for the concert?"

Rebeca gave her a quick hug. "Absolutely."

"I hear the Princeton Pedants are *guay*," Paloma said. Ethan had also heard that the band was cool, and nodded. Paloma put the tray's neck strap over her head. "I'm kind of surprised María Luisa isn't with you."

"She might join us later," Ethan said, shrugging. "Much, much later."

Paloma backed off the sidewalk. "Are the two of them at it again, Ethan?"

"Always."

"What is it this time, or don't I want to know?"

"You don't want to know. I'm not sure I know."

"Good luck, then," Paloma said with a wink. "And have a safe trip."

"I will, and thanks again. Nice to have met you."

"*Igualmente.* Enjoy the concert. Rebeca, you behave."

"I always do."

Ethan gave Rebeca the once-over. *But for how much longer?* he asked himself. He pocketed the hot sauce, but Rebeca took his surprise from him.

"I wish I had brought my purse," she said.

"I'll carry them. It's fine."

"You can't carry these around all night."

"I don't mind, really." Ethan snatched the seeds. "But I can run them home and get you a jacket."

"I'm not cold," Rebeca fibbed.

"You'll hear it from your mother if you catch a sniffle."

"Probably."

"I'd feel better if you had a jacket."

"You're sweet, but I don't want a jacket," Rebeca insisted, fussing with her high collar. She undid it, turned it back over, and then tousled her hair. "But I do need to pee. Be right back."

Ethan watched Rebeca hurry inside the bar on the corner, slide past the booth where he used to meet with his exchange studies adviser, and disappear. The restroom was in the back, but he didn't need to use it, having gone at home. Well, at the apartment, which wasn't actually home. With a little luck and a lot of scrimping and saving, it would be again soon.

His gaze wandered down Avenida Toreros and then back to the intersection. It was temporarily closed to traffic but brimming with vendors, young males wearing the obligatory attire (penny loafers, Levi's, oxford shirt, sweater tied around the neck), and cliques of brunettes who turned Ethan's head but not his heart. The guys milled about carrying lighters, chivalry in hand should a *tía buena*, hot girl, need a light. The girls were less obvious about it, but they were also on the prowl.

The gathering smelled of deep-frying churros, cologne, and cigarette smoke. There was no escaping the smoke. It stained the damp air, choked the trees, and turned the gray Plaza Mayor grayer. In Spain, breathable air seemed unnatural.

Ethan's eyes moved to the band, down the steps, and to the newspaper kiosk on the corner.

He would always remember that ordinary booth as the place where he handled his first girlie magazine. In hindsight, he should—his therapist discouraged the use of that word—have bought one that wasn't wrapped in plastic. Disappointing pages filled with shaved genitals, breast implants, and bleach-blonde hair. Such turnoffs. Live and learn. But even if he could have opened the plastic-wrapped smut before he bought it, he would have been too embarrassed to stand there flipping through it.

SUNDAY, 6 OCTOBER 2002

Las Rozas, Spain

00:43 h

Only another obsessive-compulsive could appreciate Thomas's proficiency at stripping a wet washcloth to its downy bones. And if he hadn't despised himself for the compulsion to uproot every speck of lint and head, body, and pubic hair, he might have found solace in being thoroughly competent at something.

The "parasites" were easier to spot on a light-colored rag, but even with a white rag in perfect light, an immaculate cleaning could take five or ten minutes. The washcloth in Thomas's hands was blue, and hunched over a poorly lit bathtub, he may never have been more aware that what he was doing made no sense. It never did, none of it, but the realization didn't help him stop.

Done. There's one.

Worse still, the wet bits were sticking to his fingertips, and the tub treads were so slick that, try as he might, he couldn't wipe his fingers off on them. Adding to his guilt-provoking offenses against water conservation (showers took at least twenty minutes), he turned the cold water to a trickle and rinsed one clinger after another, after another, into the strainer.

He turned off the water and tightened the knob four times. After a cleansing breath, he wrung the hell out of the washcloth, stretched it back into a perfect square, and hung it neatly on the hook. "Thank God."

He tore off a piece of toilet paper four squares long, folded the rectangle in half, and then again, and gently blew his nose. When he was done, he folded the rectangle on itself twice (horizontally and then vertically), cleaned out the tub strainer with the paper, and dropped the hairy square into the center of the toilet.

Averse to leaving fingerprints, he pulled his hands inside the shirtsleeves, pushed himself to his feet, and wiped off the rim of the tub with the right cuff thirty-seven times. He then tucked one end of the shower curtain between the tub surround and the toilet paper holder, and dragged the other end of the curtain closed, lining up the bottom corner with a grout line between two wall tiles.

Resisting the urge to recheck the knob, not to mention the bottles of shampoo, conditioner, and body wash, he cleaned his right ear eight times with the Q-tip he had set out before getting into the shower, and then swabbed his left ear eight times. He bent the swab into a "V" and let it fall into the trash from a distance that left no doubt it had made into the can.

From the travel case, the long side of which was parallel to the short side of the countertop, he took out a deodorant that from the outside appeared to be new but wasn't. He rocked off the cap, eased the stick under the bottom of the shirt, and lightly swiped each armpit, right one first, ten times. Eleven, twelve, thirteen, and fourteen swipes provoked too much anxiety. Fifteen left a caked mess in his underarm hair; the tiny balls would shed throughout the day and distract him, embarrass him, or worse, both. Using the same shower in which Lina had been naked and wet was distraction enough.

I need a snack.

His bathroom routine continued until a careful switching off of the light with a cleaned fingertip left him standing in the dark. He was done.

But there was always a precariousness to being done.

He flicked on the light and stared at the travel case. A moment later, he leaned over to the case and nudged it until its long side was absolutely, perfectly, drop-dead parallel to the short side of the countertop.

He cleaned his fingertip again and switched off the light.

Time for a snack.

He dragged himself away from the bathroom and toward the kitchen. Another routine was about to begin.

02:00 h

The Regiones neighborhood was quiet; the Plaza Mayor's trees could breathe again. Two petty thieves who had worked the concert squawked in the playhouse on the church grounds.

"The damn *policía* were everywhere," said the rag who had bullied Ethan into buying two bracelets. His frame and dark face were thin, his pockets were empty.

"Not the rich pickings from the other night," his much shorter partner said with a thick Andalusian accent. "La' fiesta' end tomorrow—today, and I'm starving." He shoved a cosmetic case into the corner and balled up his ratty jacket into a pillow. "If this goes on much longer, I won't have an ass to drag back home, and, shit, I don't want to have to do that. I guess we could beg for food—"

"I'm no beggar. To hell with that. I'll strong-arm that loser as many times as it takes, but I'm not going to beg."

"Which loser?" the short one asked.

"The American."

"The blond guy at the plaza?"

The tall one laced his fingers and lay back. "That boy had plenty of cash, and I'm sure he's got a credit card."

"But he'd cancel it as soon as he realized it was missing."

"That might take a while, and we'd drain him dry first."

"That didn't work in Majadahonda. We were lucky to get off with only a beating."

The tall one shifted to find a comfortable position for his smarting back. "Maybe I'll be second-time lucky, but even if I'm not, there's no runnin' home with my tail between my legs, that's for damn sure."

The short one curled onto his side, stomach growling. "I'm not sure which one is worse: starvation or prison." He lay there for a moment. "A night in jail I could stand, but I'm not up for doing time."

"Go home, then, you pussy."

He pounded his jacket pillow. "I'd tell you to kiss my ass if I still had one."

"And I'd cut you while you slept if I weren't so damn tired," the tall one threatened yet again. Most of the threats he made toward others involved knives or cutting.

If business had been better, they might have had a watch and known for how long they lay there in a dozy sulk, not that either of them could say or do anything at that time of night to better their situation.

An amorous male cricket finally broke the silence: *Pío, pío, pío.*

Converting cricket chirps to outdoor temperature in degrees Celsius was an old habit for the tall one. Twenty-five seconds and thirty-three chirps later, he did the math: "Thirty-three divided by three is eleven. Eleven plus four is fifteen. Fifteen degrees (fifty-nine degrees Fahrenheit)."

"That's not bad for October," the short one said. "At least we aren't hungry *and* cold."

"No, but soon fifteen will be the high temperature, not the low. And it's only going to get colder. This leaky, little house ain't going to be enough. We need coats and blankets."

"With what money?"

The cricket flirted again and then jumped toward a one-night stand. As the other two insects lay broke and hungry in their makeshift beds, neither of them could remember the last time they had attracted anything but casual heat from a woman.

08:55 h

More than forty meters higher than any other peak in the chain of rounded, indistinguishable masses of granite known as the Sierra de Guadarrama, Peñalara was the emblematic hump on the Comunidad de Madrid's northern border. In the natural park at Peñalara's summit, high-mountain flora and fauna attracted scientists and tourists alike.

On a sunny, short-sleeved afternoon many Decembers ago, Ethan had spent two cheerful hours tramping about the Parque Natural de Peñalara with his host parents before speeding on to their second home in San Rafael. At the foot of a photogenic mountain pass on the northern slopes of the Sierra, the town of San Rafael enjoyed cool summers, and its chalets were popular with Madrileños looking to beat the capital's oppressive heat.

When Ethan's relationship with his host parents became as chilly as Peñalara's snow-capped summit, he had often stared out the window of his tiny bedroom at the mountain, longing for the good old days. Just days ago, he had thought of the young Spanish Imperial Eagle his cock of a host father had seen (or said he had seen—the species was listed as "vulnerable") that day on Peñalara. Ethan doubted the bird was still alive, but he hoped that if it were, its desperate talons were hunting far away. At least for now, Ethan's pigeons were safe, roosting and bobbing around the Plaza de España as he continued to wait at the fountain for the start of today's encierro.

Down the avenida, the men who built the course every morning were at least a cigarette away from blocking off the side street, so Álvaro and Rebeca weren't late. At least by Spanish standards. Ethan swallowed the last bite of his baguette of cooked ham, balled up the foil, and pocketed it.

He had tossed and turned most of the night, the sleepless minutes outnumbering the pipas hulls in the cup beside him. The spicy treats were much too valuable to waste on something as usual as a bout of insomnia, but he had popped enough of them as he lay propped against his pillow to get a stiff neck. He began to stretch it, tilting his head side to side as he focused on a distant roof to keep from getting dizzy.

Poking above the roof like a distorted vessel beyond the horizon of a flat sea was Peñalara's summit. Ethan began to think of his mother and the ashes he had spread and tucked back in Virginia's Blue Ridge Mountains. *What's the weather like today at Porter's Mountain Overlook?* he asked himself, not all that interested in the answer. *I wonder if the boulder has snow on it. Mom loved it when everything was turned white.*

The weather in the Virginia mountains was a matter for tomorrow, or the day after, when he wasn't whipped by jetlag. Today, the peaks of Madrid's Sierra de Guadarrama were veiled: An approaching storm system was threatening to put a sloppy end to the fiestas.

Ethan hurried to the nearby newspaper kiosk, took a free copy of the *Fiestas De San Miguel* 2002 brochure, and returned to the fountain. He flipped through the brochure, found the schedule, and read to himself the events for the rest of the day: *an exhibition of radio-controlled stunt planes, a novillada* (bullfight with two- to three-year-old bulls), *the closing ceremony at town hall, a coordinated display of firecrackers and fireworks on the outskirts.* He glanced at the veiled mountain peaks. *Bad weather will likely affect two of the events, three if the novillada is cancelled because of wind.*

Rain annoyed bullfighters, wind got them killed.

Ethan closed the brochure and left it on the rim of the fountain for someone else. Luckily, his plans included none of the scheduled events, and he had high hopes for a good day, and higher ones for a tension-free evening. Asking María Luisa to be his platonic date for Óscar's dinner had seemed a good idea at the time. If she and Rebeca hadn't killed each other before supper, he might still get to savor Taberna de Regiones's house potatoes in peace.

It's not like Rebeca and Álvaro to be this late, he told himself. *Where are they?* He scanned the plaza, the gazebo, Café Sol, the arcaded passageways, the antique shop. His thoughts turned to the wooden box that was waiting to be picked up, to the tape that would have a beautiful home after he did. And then to his mother. "Miss you, Mom," he whispered.

If Ethan were being honest with himself, he probably missed the idea of her more. Adult children didn't need a mother, and his had struggled with the transition from being the air inside her little boy's balloon to feeling like the string that hung from it when it floated away.

Despite her psychologist's insistence that she would never have gotten better as long as she stayed married, she had gotten so much worse after the divorce. Sulking, cryptic comments, backhanded compliments ("I wish I could be as selfish as you" was Ethan's favorite), self-created chaos, general lack of boundaries, especially the constant phone calls—more unwanted intrusions, even the ringing was a damnation.

As far as Ethan was concerned, his mother's therapist had been a quack, and the only thing that had gotten "better" was his father's bad back because of the ergonomic bed he had bought after leaving the family home.

Of all the things that hadn't gotten "better," Ethan's mother depending on him like a second husband had been the worst. He had faulted her for treating him that way, and he had hated himself for enabling it. Between the blurry time of her filing for divorce and the moment she drew her last breath, their mother-son relationship had been as harmonious as a twisted fork and a bent spoon hanging by threads on a whimsical wind chime.

And though she was gone now, Ethan's mental scars lingered. His relationship with his father ebbed and flowed. Ethan's behavior frequently left his dad scratching his head.

Sorry for being a mystery to you, Dad, Ethan thought. *Sorry for—*

"Snap out of it!" Rebeca urged with a poke.

Embarrassed, Ethan managed to smile. "It must be my turn to daydream."

"Apparently," she said, tying a red handkerchief around her neck. "Are you ready to do this thing?"

"As ready as I'll ever be," Ethan said, gently pulling out the strands of Rebeca's hair caught in the knot she had tied. "Just waiting for Álvaro."

Rebeca tousled her hair. "Thanks, and Álvaro's not coming."

He resisted the urge to ask her if Álvaro had already 'come.' "Why not?"

"He's . . . tired."

"But I don't know what the devil I'm doing out there. He's my escort."

"Today, I'll have to do."

"You're running?"

Rebeca grinned. "Like a gazelle."

"It's been *years* since you've run."

She adjusted the handkerchief. "Like a fashionable gazelle."

"Well, I'm no gazelle. That's why Álvaro—"

"He's at home in bed, so you'll have to trust me."

"I trust you," Ethan said, "but—"

"I know what I'm doing," she said with a wink.

"But I don't do this often enough to do it right."

"By 'do it right,' do you mean paying as much attention to the other runners as you do to the bulls? Hugging the barriers on the corners, staying down if you fall down? And not touching the bulls or running too closely behind or in front of them?"

"You forgot eating a good breakfast, smartass." He showed her the balled up foil.

"And getting a good night's sleep, but guessing from the dark circles under your eyes, it's too late for that."

He tossed the ball at her. "You know me too well."

She shoved the foil into her pocket and began to pull him by the shirt. "I know you, I know me, and I know how to keep us safe."

"Okay, but if you get me killed, I'll never speak to you again."

09:50 h

If Ethan's mother were looking down on him from Heaven, she probably couldn't bear watching what he was doing in the plaza de toros. And she certainly would have disapproved of the tradition that gave him the opportunity to do it.

Rebeca's mother was at home, dressing for church, and she, too, would have feared for her daughter's safety. But she had never given a second thought to the tradition of releasing a vaquilla into the ring after a bullfight or an encierro so that the locals could mess around with it.

A young bull trotted out of the toril gate. His laughably mismatched horns had deemed him unsuitable for fighting, even in third-category plazas, but his breeding made the scene about to play out both a fair fight and a cruel example of Spain's addiction to tradition.

Ethan retied his dusty sneakers without taking his eyes off the vaquilla, which charged indiscriminately here and there with youthful vigor. The animal would be killed before day's end, but before a rifle was put to his forehead, he could do some damage. Rebeca hopped off the running board that jutted out from the barrera and leaned down to Ethan. "Don't forget that a vaquilla killed Antonio Bienvenida," she warned him as her hair fell onto his head.

Ethan still marveled at the irony of one of the more brilliant toreros in history being killed *after* retiring from the ring, while testing vaquillas on a friend's *finca*, rural estate.

"Where he was killed isn't far from here," Rebeca said, wrapping her ponytail. "On the road to El Escorial, past the ranch where you had your picture taken straddling that adorable calf with the blaze that looked like an *estrella fugaz*." Shooting star: It had been the term of that day.

"And where we ate that succulent paella," Ethan added as the vaquilla ran a younger and faster man than he back to the barrera.

"It was *arroz valenciana*, not paella."

"I still get those two confused."

"Paella's made with white wine, and it's baked until the rice absorbs the liquid but is still firm," Rebeca explained. "Arroz valenciana is cooked on the stove in an earthen casserole, and the rice is soft and creamy. The rancher's wife stirred the dish, remember?"

"I was trying to keep up with the conversation between Álvaro and our host," Ethan said, watching the vaquilla sweep along the barrera toward them. His heart started to pound. "I'm not sure what the rancher's wife was doing, but both dishes contain seafood."

Rebeca pulled him toward the center of the ring; her first instinct had always been to protect him. "Paella's a fancy seafood dish; arroz valenciana is peasant food."

"For poor folks like me."

"You're rich in other ways, ones that matter. Besides, money rarely brings happiness."

"Trite but true," Ethan agreed. "Boy, you're on a roll today."

"And I'm just getting started," she said, testing her footing.

"Where do you think you're going?" Ethan asked as she stepped away from him and toward the vaquilla.

As most bulls do, this one had begun to favor a certain part of the ring, but it had far too much energy to stand in one place for long. It trotted out of its querencia, stopped, looked left, right, and then left again. Responding instinctively, it pursued an invader for a short distance, paused, spun, and then trotted toward its original spot, but stopped short, leaving it a stone's throw from Rebeca.

Ethan scooted toward her. "I told Álvaro I would keep you safe."

"When did you tell him that?"

"Yesterday afternoon, when I came to get you in La Rinconera."

"So you haven't spoken to him this morning?" she asked.

"No, but you said you were just kidding about messing with the vaquilla."

"I was, but that was yesterday," she said, adjusting her ponytail as the vaquilla watched. "Today's a new day. A good day."

"A good day to get yourself killed," he said. "I don't care how crazy looking those horns are, they'll do the job." Ethan couldn't read women or bulls, but something told him that the animal, which had turned away from them, was about to do something predictable. He sidled up to Rebeca. "I'm not sure why you're determined to do this, but we're doing it together," he said. "If he charges, run *that* way, and I'll run *that* way," he continued, pointing in opposite directions. "He can't catch both of us."

Rebeca grinned. "Let's see how close we can get."

"You're going to be the death of me."

"Not today."

They approached the vaquilla from behind, marching side by side to find where fearlessness ended and foolishness began. At some six meters away, they paused, but then continued forward, just to see how far they could go. At five meters, Ethan's inner voice spoke to him. At four meters, it shouted at him. At three meters, it pleaded with him, and the adrenaline rush was almost paralyzing. Ethan knew where foolishness began. They both did, but they took an imprudent step forward. And then another.

They had inched to within two meters of the vaquilla's hindquarters when the animal turned its head and saw them. Rebeca stepped left. Ethan slid right. With the vaquilla's angry snort, the chase was on.

Ethan made a beeline for the nearest burladero, without even a glance at his pursuer. The murmur of the spectators crescendoed to a gasp. As he darted into the safety of the callejón, the looks on the spectators' faces told him that his escape had been as narrow as the opening behind the burladero. Ethan's heart was pounding.

It wasn't the first time he had put himself at the mercy of a bull's animal instinct, but as he stood there, watching Rebeca hurry across the ring, he swore it would be his last. "I said you'd be the death of me," he panted.

"And I said that it wouldn't be today," she answered with a hug. "So unless I can talk to the dead, I was right."

"Well, you certainly can talk. And talk and talk, but I'm not dead, just lucky."

"It was touch and go there for a moment, though."

"Tell me about it."

Rebeca's smile faded, and after hugging him again, her voice took on a serious, almost apologetic tone. "A vaquilla can run faster than you can," she said. "I thought you knew that."

"I did, I do."

"Then why did you run in a straight line? You have to confuse it."

"I guess I didn't have time to think."

Making figures in the air that served as visual aids for her impromptu lesson, she continued: "To escape from a wild animal, you have to zigzag."

"We ran straight down the course during the encierro."

"The herding instinct of bulls is powerful; they simply follow the one in front of it. That's why they use bullocks to lead them down the course."

Ethan nodded.

"And what happens when one of the bulls gets separated from the herd?"

"Watch out."

"No shit," Rebeca agreed. "Well, vaquillas are just smaller versions of the monsters that were fought yesterday afternoon."

Embarrassed and humbled, Ethan nodded again. "Well, you don't need to worry because I've just decided to retire."

"You don't have to stop having fun. Just be careful, that's all."

"No, I think I'm done. Besides, I don't know if you've noticed, but we're the oldest ones out here."

"I see that," Rebeca said, taking a look around. Standing in its querencia, the vaquilla was being pestered by chavales whose bravery was waxing as the young bull's energy and interest were waning. "But I don't really care what they think, do you?"

"Not really."

"So why stop?"

"I'm a curiosity, being American and all, but in your case, the neighbors might think you're a bit of a fool."

"As a woman out here with all these boys, I'm a curiosity, too."

"There are a lot more girls than there used to be," Ethan said, "but you are the only woman out here. And while we're on the subject, *why* are you out here? You haven't run with the bulls in years, and you certainly haven't messed with a vaquilla, though you've had plenty of chances."

"I told you that today is a new and good day."

"But I don't know what you mean by that."

Rebeca took her hair out of a ponytail, tousled it, and placed the scrunchy around her wrist. "Things are winding down here. I'm ready to go if you are."

"We can leave whenever you want," he said, taking one last look at the vaquilla, which was scrabbling the sand. "I've retired, remember?"

"We've both retired."

"Álvaro will be glad to hear—"

"It's easier if we cut across," she interrupted, eyeing the crowded callejón and the exit they had used yesterday afternoon. She reentered the ring through the opening behind the burladero. "*Vámonos.*"

"Right behind you, guapa."

Hugging the barrera, they weaved their way through the tweens and teenagers on the periphery and crossed the ring without incident. They slipped behind the burladero and into the section of the callejón where a bullfighter had relieved himself during yesterday's corrida. The area still had a slight smell of urine. They exited under the stands.

"Are you ever going to tell me what you meant by today being 'a new and good day'?" Ethan asked Rebeca as they left the plaza and the crowd behind.

"Guess."

"I'm almost afraid to."

"Go ahead, guess. Or talk to Álvaro, but I'd rather you didn't."

"I knew it," Ethan said.

"Knew what?"

He leaned into her. "You finally did it, didn't you?"

"Did what?"

"IT," he whispered, although there was no one around to hear. "You know, dip the churro."

"What, have I lost that 'hard look' virgins have?" she asked.

"I'm not sure *what* look you have."

"I'm not sure either," Rebeca said as the veiled sun peeked out from behind the clouds for the last time, "but this is a day to remember."

10:45 h

Aided by an umbrella walking cane that was a shade darker than her short-sleeved sheath and matching shawl, Sra. Navas crossed Avenida de la Constitución and continued on to the church grounds. Pensive, she tapped her way up the flights of steps that Sr. Serrano had carried her down on their wedding day. Time and familiarity had dulled the pitter-patter of her heart when she was in his arms now, but she still loved him and the homey comfort that came with his embrace. His days of playfully swooping her up and carrying her around were long behind him, but as she slowly topped the steep steps, she would not have minded turning back the clock, just for a moment.

If she had paused to look over her shoulder, she would have seen the weather front creeping up on the Sierra. Her arthritic knees had been telling her the same thing. The joints ground and cracked, but the pain was nothing compared to that of losing a child. She tapped across the courtyard, making a point to acknowledge each churchgoer she met in some way, even the old man who was shuffling by.

She had always enjoyed the crunch of gravel underfoot, and as she reached the church's rear nave doors, she was more content than anxious. Before going inside, she glanced at the grouping of beech saplings near the corner of the courtyard. Among the trees was the picnic table where Ethan used to tutor Rebeca. Sra. Navas sighed wistfully, smiled, and then opened one of the red doors.

As she stepped inside the church, the vigil lights burning near the statue of San Miguel danced inside their devotional holders. Lit by friends and neighbors with votive prayers for themselves or on behalf of others, the candles cast a flickering light of hope and protection that had once soothed the devout mother of a baby with Reye's Syndrome. But even *if* Sra. Navas's prayers had ridden up to Heaven on the candles' heat, God in his "infinite wisdom" had chosen to let the flame be extinguished by her mournful tears, which flowed openly, carrying away with them her loyalty to the bargain.

In the years since Félix's death, Sra. Navas had shed most of her tears in private, behind a closed bedroom door that hid more than just her sorrow.

She had cried this morning, too, and then dressed herself in beige, a blah color, like her interest in going to mass. But she had gone anyway, and now the mother of a long-dead baby stood there, still holding the handle to the red door of the house of God.

The aroma of burning incense greeted her, but she felt anything but welcome.

12:00 h

Marisa's chest heaved as her deliberate sigh broke the silence. Her breasts were ample, unlike Lina's, but it was now painfully clear to her that Thomas had little desire to touch them, even through her shirt. Watching him fidget in the corner of her bedroom, she sensed his anxiety, which was curiously both better *and* worse this morning. Despite last night's setback, she wasn't ready to abandon her dream. "Can't you at least look at me?" she asked him.

"I *can*," Thomas said, making infinitesimal adjustments to the figurines on her bookcase, "but it's getting harder and harder."

Marisa smacked her lips. "Speaking of getting harder—"

"I'm out of here if you don't stop doing that."

She threw up her hands. "Fine, I'll stop."

"I'm not kidding."

"Jeez, I was just playing around."

He nudged a porcelain swan. "Somehow, I doubt it."

"I'm done. Really. But please turn around. I hate talking to the back of you."

He nudged the swan again and slowly turned. "I can't take any more of that shit right now, got it?"

Marisa gave him a playful frown. "My bad."

"There's too much going on right now. Not a good time."

"Come here, and let's talk about it."

Thomas shook his head. "I'm fine here."

"I'll be good," she promised, crossing her heart. "Come here and sit down, you baby."

Fighting the urge to turn back to the swan, he tugged on the bracelet four times and took a seat on the edge of the bed.

"I won't bite," she said and patted the bedspread next to her.

He threw her a look but stayed put, saying nothing.

"Tell me what's going on in that head of yours."

"Anxiety, confusion, thoughts I can't shake, a bit of self-loathing—the norm, and then some."

There was nothing playful about her frown. "I can only imagine."

Thomas ran his finger over the scar on his wrist. "I doubt you can. Lord, I hope you never have to go through this."

"Help me to understand, then," she said, reaching for his hand and placing it between hers.

"I can't."

"You can't, or you won't?"

Thomas let his hand linger before withdrawing it. He crossed his arms in a hopeful gesture of self-restraint. "I just can't."

"Aren't we beyond playing these stupid games?" she asked with a tilt of the head.

"Yes."

"Then talk to me, please. You're making me nervous."

"*You're* nervous?"

Marisa stared at his crossed arms. "So this is about going home?"

"Good guess, but—"

"You're not thinking about hurting yourself again, are you?" Her voice was trembling.

"No."

"Promise me you'll never do this again to yourself," she pleaded, uncrossing his arms as she took him by the wrist. "Promise me."

He wanted to resist. "Okay."

"I couldn't take it if anything ever happened to you."

"I absolutely, definitely promise," Thomas said with tenuous sincerity.

"But the thought does cross your mind from time to time, doesn't it?"

Slipping from her grip, he reached again for his wrist. "I'd be lying if I said it didn't."

"Well, at least you're being honest," Marisa said, inching closer to him. "I know what being at home does to you."

"I get *so* much worse."

"I know."

"I don't think even *you* would believe what I have to do to make it through the day."

"I have some idea."

"How can I . . ."

"How can you *what*?"

Thomas's eyes met Marisa's before focusing on the swan. "Even if *someone* wants to spend her life with me, how can I let her? Real life has been like death for me; going home has been like going home to die. It just wouldn't be fair to ask *someone* to put up with that."

Marisa's heart began to race as the words tumbled out of Thomas's mouth. She pushed her luck. "Are you asking me to go with you? Because I would, you know. I'd move in a heartbeat. I could help you. Cook and clean for you, do all those things that plague you. It would be *my* choice, so you wouldn't have to feel guilty."

The thought of even a sympathetic and willing invader in his "home" sent an anxiety-provoking shot of adrenaline down the back of Thomas's legs and into his feet. "Down, girl."

"Or I could give you a little time to get back and get settled, and then join you."

His feet still pounding, Thomas shook his head. "If I don't go home, I don't have to return to that life. I don't hate myself nearly as much when I'm *here*."

"So stay."

"With whom?"

"Stay right where you are."

He shot her a look that needed no explanation. "I'm pushing my luck as it is."

"I know," she said, gritting her teeth.

"I'm screwed either way. How could you afford to move anyway?"

"You're giving me whiplash."

"You sh—oughta be in here," Thomas said, pounding himself on the head.

Marisa's ample chest heaved again. She arched her back and scooted closer. "Let's take this one step at a time, okay?"

"Sure."

"Do you want to stay, or do you want to go?"

He answered without hesitation: "I'd love to stay, but—"

"No buts," Marisa said.

"But given the situation, maybe going home is the better option."

"And if you go, do you want me to go with you, either now or later?"

"I'm not sure I'm going."

Marisa threw her hands up again. "You're making my head spin, and not in a good way."

"Sorry."

"So where's the money coming from if you're staying?"

"Oh, I can get the money. Or the credit," Thomas whispered, his mind wandering back to yesterday afternoon at the Plaza de España, to the "fucking loser" who had been bullied into buying bracelets. "There's always force."

13:30 h

Ethan's reminiscences of his short-lived college days were few, and they involved geology, not Spanish. There was nothing pleasurable about recalling intimidated classmates whispering behind his back or cash-strapped, straight-D coeds inviting him to hop *onto* but not *into* their textbook-strewn beds. Bartering tutoring for sex might have gotten him some action, but that just wasn't him.

Although the smartest *tío*, guy, in the classroom hadn't soured on the Spanish language, the study of it had left a frustrating taste in his mouth that had gotten as old as the rocks he had studied in geology.

In those stony masses, the history of the Earth was recorded, and he had listened with eager ears to professors lecture about that recording. But on Tuesday afternoons, in an earthy basement laboratory and on an outcropping a college bus ride away, Ethan's fingers had been like phonograph needles, tracking the faults and fissures to tell the story by himself. The first sounds had been scratchy at best, but his mistakes had been productive. Bit by bit, he had become acquainted with minerals—the building blocks of rocks—and together they had cleaned up the recording.

Geologically speaking, his best friends were the ten reference minerals of Mohs Hardness Scale, or the "Scale of 'Scratchability,'" as Ethan called it. Generally speaking, his best friends were Rebeca and María Luisa, with whom he now sat listening to their parents hash out the day's headlines over a first course of *potaje de garbanzos*, garbanzo bean soup.

Although Ethan hadn't tested to see how well Sr. Serrano's skull resisted scratching, it was obvious that in the face of most arguments, Pedro's head was at least as hard as topaz. When it came to his beliefs and prejudices, the man's stubbornness rivaled corundum, if not diamond. It was fitting that his name meant "rock," but he wasn't the only hardheaded Serrano. However, he was the one who occupied the seat at the head of the table. The current topic of conversation was beginning to bring out the harder side of him. "So I told Jesús to give that boy of his a swift kick in the ass," he said, spooning a thin round of chorizo.

Sra. Navas slurped her *potaje*. She had cooked it slower and longer than usual, making it more of a stew than a soup, and added a few collard greens. She glanced around and was happy to see that it was a hit. "Don't be so hard on him, Pedro. It hasn't been that long."

"That long since what?" María Luisa dared to interrupt.

"Since Jesús's wife died," her mother said.

Rebeca and María Luisa exchanged looks, and then with Ethan. "Jesús Hierro?"

"No, Jesús Martín," Sr. Serrano snorted at his older daughter. "Don't you ever talk to the neighbors?"

"What kind of trouble has his son been giving him?" Sra. Navas asked before they could wreck the meal she had worked so hard to prepare.

"He's a bum."

"A bum? Isn't that a bit harsh, considering what he's gone through?"

"He's quit playing fútbol and just lies around all day. Jesús says he's got a bit of a gut. Hell, he's probably too soft to rejoin the team, and that's *if* the coach would want him back."

"Ethan, my dear, can I get you some more water?"

He shook his head. "I'm fine, thanks."

"The death of a mother is a hard thing to get over," Sra. Navas said. "If I had to guess, I'd say he's depressed."

Sr. Serrano gave Ethan a pat on the back, and then shook him by the shoulder. "This guy's not lying around."

The kids exchanged another look.

Sra. Navas reached for a piece of bread and tore it in half. "Each of us reacts in our own way. Each of our brains reacts in its own way. Don't be so quick to judge the boy," she said, patting at the thick broth. "If he's ill, he needs help, just like someone with a *physical* illness."

"What he needs to do is bust his ass to find a job that will keep him too busy to be depressed." Staring over the glass at his older daughter, he took a swig of mineral water. "The last thing Spain needs is another mentally ill parasite."

María Luisa tore the spoon out of her mouth. "Or another unfeeling hardhead who thinks he knows everything about everything."

"I've had more than enough of you lately—"

"You don't know the first thing about depression. And, yes, it's an illness, and it's as real as any physical illness."

"When did you become a doctor? The last time I checked, you were a college dropout."

"At least I gave it a go, unlike you, *professor*."

"*I've* been too busy working to put food in *your* mouth."

Ethan gave Rebeca a gentle kick under the table. "Not the time for jokes," he whispered.

"I'm not getting involved," she said. "She's doing a fine job of digging her own grave."

"Shut up, Rebeca," María Luisa snapped. "You're one to talk."

Wisely refusing to take the bait, Rebeca spooned her last bit of potaje and slurped it loudly without saying a word.

"Let's change the subject, shall we?" Sra. Navas asked.

Finishing her bowl, María Luisa nodded. "Yes, let's. Why discuss something that's actually important? When Jesús's son kills himself, we can revisit the topic."

"You're walking on shaky ground," her father growled.

"No one is going to commit suicide," Sra. Navas said. "One of us will talk to Jesús. Isn't that right, Pedro?"

"What for?"

"Everyone needs a hand every once in a while."

Sr. Serrano pushed away his empty bowl. "He'll politely tell you to mind your own business."

"Perhaps, but it's still the friendly thing to do." Sra. Navas glanced around the table. "Has everyone finished?" she asked, hoping to carry away the tension with the dishes.

"I'm finished," Rebeca said, running a thirsty bite of bread around her bowl.

María Luisa finished chewing. "Done."

"Done for," Rebeca whispered.

"Me, too," Ethan said with another kick for Rebeca.

Sra. Navas reached for his bowl. "I hope you liked it."

"Delicious," he said and patted his bottle of hot sauce. "It didn't even need this." He started to get up. "Let me help you."

"No, you sit. I'll help you, Mamá," María Luisa said.

Pleasantly surprised by the offer, Sra. Navas thanked her. The two women began to clear the table. "I'll be happy to give you the recipe so you can make it when you get home," she told Ethan.

He gave her a peck on the cheek and sat back down.

15:26 h

Obsessional and compulsional reasoning had run through his head during the night. He had tweaked the premises and written them down:

> *My brain is a liar;*
> *I despise myself for listening to it;*
> *I can't stop, no matter what I do or how hard I try;*
> *even the idea of getting better chokes me with fear;*
> *the meds gave me boobs and made me a zombie;*
> *a part of me is dead to the possibility of ever*
> *being happy, but I don't deserve to be;*
> *who could ever love me?*

The paragraph's rounded shape was intentional, and the premises supported the chilling conclusion that he had a snowball's chance in hell of being with the one he loved. Regardless, he was desperate to escape the reality of having to leave Las Rozas, and, like every other avalanche victim trapped beneath the snow, he was looking for a way out.

He read the paragraph again and neatly folded the sheet of paper. Struggling to put it away in his button-flap pocket, he watched several cars and then a glass repair company van carrying a large mirror pass by. A reflection caught his attention. He stared at the blond hair. *Fucking loser . . .*

Several minutes later, he grabbed the blond hair. "Hey, asshole."

15:30 h

Sra. Navas had always believed that María Luisa was conceived during a lightning visit to Catalonian apple country, in the back of a sedan pulled off a road that was embraced by trees laden with clusters of pinkish-white blossoms. She had been on top, unabashedly stripped to the waist and pantiless beneath her skirt, riding Sr. Serrano's erection in ways that would have gotten her unmarried self condemned to a nunnery if they had been caught. And he, panting into her titillating breasts and cupping her naked backside, had been trying to keep from disappointing his new bride by coming too soon.

They had waited until she began to show to tell the family. When Sra. Navas had been asked by her aunt when she had conceived, she had lied with flushed cheeks and a straight, almost apologetic face about the strictly procreative purpose of *relaciones sexuales* during a tender moment in a hostel near Barcelona. "Tender" had also been a lie: There had been nothing soft about the most erotic moment of Sra. Navas's life.

It wasn't the first time Sr. Serrano had come in a car. She had attended to his needs a couple of times, at the end of a date, when he got *that* look on his face. She knew why she had done it, and had no regrets, then or now, after thirty-plus years of living, learning, and losing.

She had stopped bowing to guilt, for the most part, but sadly and stubbornly, appearances still mattered. She put on a happy face that masked her uneasiness as she approached María Luisa's bedroom. The know-it-all who had grown from the seed planted that night in the orchard was zipping a rain jacket that used to be much too big on her.

"Ready to go to the BurgoCentro?" she asked, smiling at her daughter.

María Luisa slipped her purse over her shoulder. "Ready."

"I'm glad you're coming with me."

"Papá's back at work," María Luisa said, "but I need a break from Rebeca."

"We won't be gone too long if my knees hold up. It will give you time to clear your head before dinner."

"Your knees will be fine, but let's not rush."

Sra. Navas gestured toward the closet. "Do you know what you're going to wear tonight?"

"It's already picked out, but don't let me forget to buy a lipstick to match the dress."

"I'll add it to the list," her mother said, tapping her head. "My knees are shot but not my memory. Oh, you two are going to have such a wonderful time."

"We better; it's our last hurrah before he leaves tomorrow."

"And the dinner's at Taberna de Regiones?"

"At nine o'clock." María Luisa's words trailed off as her mind wandered. "I'm surprised Ethan hasn't changed his mind and invited Rebeca instead, given the way I've been acting lately."

"Ethan's your biggest fan. He'd never do that to you."

María Luisa fumbled through her purse. "I'm still surprised."

"I'm not," Sra. Navas fibbed. "Come on, let's go."

"Let's," she said, already a few steps behind her mother.

"Have a good walk," Rebeca shouted with a mouth full of toothpaste from the bathroom between the front bedroom and the kitchen. She spat and rinsed, but stayed put.

Sra. Navas stepped around a pair of sandals lying near the front door. "We'll be back in a while," she shouted back, grabbing the umbrella walking cane propped in the corner. "Chain the door. And move these sandals before someone trips."

"I will. Take your time. One of you could use the exercise."

Biting her tongue, María Luisa opened the door for her mother.

"Good girl," Sra. Navas whispered as she tapped past her.

"I'm not in the mood for a shouting match." She pulled the door closed by the dummy knob and locked it.

"I'm glad you're coming with me," Sra. Navas said again.

María Luisa took her mother by the arm, as any loving Spanish daughter would. She escorted her down the stairs and through the vestibule.

"Did you get the mail yesterday?" Sra. Navas asked, tapping through another door opened for her.

María Luisa shut the wormwood door. "No, but—"

"I did," Rebeca said from the balcony.

"What now?" her sister asked, annoyed.

"I just wanted to tell you that . . . I have a lipstick that might match the dress, if it's the one I remember."

María Luisa stared at Rebeca. "And?"

"And you're welcome to borrow it for your 'last hurrah.'"

"That's generous of you," Sra. Navas said. "Isn't that generous of her, hija?"

"Couldn't you have mentioned that *before* we left?"

Rebeca shrugged her shoulders. "I guess. Sorry."

"You're in a rare mood this afternoon," María Luisa said. "What, did you and Álvaro finally—"

"Thank your sister, and let's go."

"Thank you," María Luisa said matter-of-factly.

"Happy to help."

"I doubt it." Her words were tinged with suspicion.

"We're going," Sra. Navas said. "And, Rebeca . . ."

"Yes, Mamá."

"We're going to have a talk later," her mother said, tapping her umbrella cane on the sidewalk.

Rebeca leaned over the railing. "About what?"

"Later."

"When?"

"I think while Ethan and María Luisa are at the dinner would be a good time."

"I'll be here."

"Yes, you'll be *here*, and I'll be *there*," María Luisa bragged, gesturing in the direction of Taberna. "And if need be, I'll go with Ethan to pick up his box."

"You do that."

"I will," María Luisa smirked and then left with her mother on her arm.

Reveling in her self-restraint and in the sight of the seeing them go, Rebeca watched Sra. Navas and María Luisa walk up Avenida de la Constitución and pause to let a car turn out of a side street. As they did, Rebeca scanned the gloomy sky and let her eyes fall on the cross atop the tapering spire on the church's bell tower.

The highest point in the neighborhood, it would catch the first raindrops and be cleansed of the bird droppings corroding it. *In time, what you leave behind is washed into memory*, she remembered someone saying. Rebeca leaned again over the railing, blew a kiss into La Rinconera, where Álvaro's shift was ending, and hopped like a red-breasted robin back inside the apartment.

15:36 h

Thomas stood with an empty plastic bag in his hand, venom on his tongue, and malice in his heart. "You're such a fucking loser," he said, glancing around, "and I'm going to reach in there and do it, so help me God."

Ironically, if there was a God, and the perfect being had truly "created man in His own image," there was no need to bring Him into it: Thomas wasn't His creation.

15:45 h

The scent of coconut body wash lingered on Rebeca's skin. Loose, tousled waves of hair lightly brushed her shoulders. Her bow-shaped lips glistened with a balm, but no makeup had touched her Mediterranean face.

Under an off-shoulder top and sassy blue jeans, her favorite bra and panties were finally ready to be properly introduced. Her lightly dimpled thighs were high on palmfuls of caffeinated cellulite cream, but the rest of her slim, some would say enviable legs jittered without having drunk a drop. The soles of her high-arched feet, which she had always hated, were tacky with hydrating lotion, and they stuck to the floor of the bedroom that had been hers since she was born.

But her spirit was unbound and ready to grab life by the horns. For the first time in forever, she felt beautiful and self-confident, and was pleased with the head-to-toe reflection in the mirror, even the sight of her breasts, which like her, were a handful. *Álvaro was right. My ass looks great.*

Her Spanish blood was racing as she faced herself again. She poked at the condom already in her fifth pocket. *This is so not the time for an oops baby*, she told herself with a glance at her unwound alarm clock, *but it's definitely time for this piece of ass to get moving.*

She crossed herself without hesitation, switched off the light, and hurried as quickly as her sticky feet would let her past the master bedroom and María Luisa's "dungeon" and into the front hallway. The salón's French doors were open, as were the ones to the balcony.

The brightness in her eyes flickered as she collected herself near the front door. The wall clock's soothing tick-tock, which everyone else seemed to ignore, was a whisper of its usual self. *That's what happens when you forget to wind it, Rebeca*, she scolded herself. But there was nothing she could do about it now. Run-down hands could not be trusted when minutes could make all the difference in the world, so she went to check the clock on the electric stove.

Nodding an "I thought so," she did a quick bit of guesstimation, sighing with relief that there was still plenty of time. She glided out of the kitchen and up the hall.

She hadn't seen Ethan since lunch, and his room was quiet as she knocked on the door. There was no answer, but she knocked again. "It's me," she said.

"Un momento, por favor."

She waited patiently and then tucked her hair behind her ear and put it to the door. "I need to tell you something, and I don't want to talk through this door," she said, listening to him close a long zipper.

"Come in," he stuttered, on his knees. "I'm just trying to find room for all the stuff I've bought."

Rebeca took in the scene. "I see that. But if you can stop for a moment."

"Vale," he managed to say, choking up into an open suitcase, and then awkwardly got to his feet. "What can I do for you, guapa?"

And as he turned around her suspicions were confirmed. Her

bare feet stepped toward him. "What's wrong?"

"*Nada*," he lied, unable to catch his breath.

"I don't believe you."

"I'm fine. Really."

"You can't hide anything from me. Come on, out with it."

He could hardly look at her.

"You disappeared after lunch. Did something happen to you?"

"You could say that."

"So what was it?"

It was getting even harder to look at her. With a glance at his mess, he turned around and faced the window. The world outside was getting grayer. "It's embarrassing."

"I promise not to laugh," she said and sidled up to him. "I would never laugh."

"And it's complicated."

"I'll try to keep up."

He pulled the belt away from the wall and eased the shutter down with both hands, leaving it open a few inches. At night, when it and the door were closed, the room was as dark as the shadow of a matte black bull, and he often woke with the terrifying sensation of having gone blind. Until the moment passed, it was overwhelming, much like this one. But this afternoon his eyesight was perfect. "Aren't you on your way out or something?"

"Something, but I've got time. Turn around and talk to me, *por fa*."

It doesn't make any difference now, he told himself. As he turned around to face her, his eyes dropped to the floor. "I don't want your parents to know."

"Not a word."

"Promise?"

"My lips are sealed," Rebeca said, grabbing and lifting his chin. "Out with it."

"There's . . ."

"There's what? I'll get it out of you one way or another."

"There's . . . a guy . . ."

And once he began he didn't stop until he had told her everything. As she had promised, there was no laughter, only anger, but it wasn't directed at him. And as he was finishing, she couldn't have cared less about how the afternoon was *supposed* to go. Although he didn't ask her for help, she knew exactly what to do.

17:05 h

Except for the industrious Sr. Serrano, who was downstairs *cascando*, chatting, about the obscene amount of money he was going to owe an electrician, the rest of the family was home. Sra. Navas lay in bed, awake but resting. Rebeca had changed clothes and was lost in her reflection. Ethan fumbled in his suitcases.

María Luisa drowsed on the couch in the salón. The balcony doors were shut, the television set was off, the lights were low. The room was hers. Oblivious to the recent breach of the status quo, she wanted to capture the peace and quiet and guard them in her memory. Or in a box as beautiful as the one being held for Ethan.

But she hadn't seen him since arriving home from the BurgoCentro with the perfect shade of lipstick to match her dress. Even if Rebeca *did* have a matching lipstick, she wasn't going to borrow a damn thing from her. María Luisa thought again about Ethan's box. *I wonder whether he's already gone to get it.*

The thought sparked a quick debate about the pros and cons of knocking on his door to find out, and then a much longer one about whether to ask about his mother's tape altogether. *I don't want to push or to pry.* Yeah, right. If she had her way, he would have already listened to it, out of respect for the woman. For his own good. And with her help, of course: You didn't have to be a buttinsky to be curious about a message left by a dying mother to her distant son.

Maybe he's already listened to it, and that's why he's been so quiet this afternoon. Or maybe he's doing it right now. She craned over the back of the couch to listen for any sign of life coming through the wall. "*Ni pío*—Not a peep."

Her neck stayed stretched until the aroma of *tortilla de patatas*, a thick egg, onion, and potato frittata, beckoned everyone to the kitchen for the late-afternoon snack. Reluctantly, María Luisa shifted herself back into a comfortable position. She was quickly ensconced again in her solitude until the ringing of a desk phone interrupted her thoughts. *The phone's always for Rebeca anyway*, she told herself, intending not to answer it. But on the off chance that Ethan's father was calling, she couldn't just let it ring. "*Dígame*," she said into the receiver.

"Is Rebeca there?" a female voice said.

"May I ask who's calling?"

"This is Paloma."

"One moment," she said and covered the receiver. "Rebeca!"

"Coming," Rebeca yelled back, marching in stocking feet past the kitchen. Two slight, dry coughs preceded her entrance. "Who is it?"

María Luisa pushed the receiver at her. "Paloma," she said, stretching the cord. "Chat away, I'm going to the bathroom and then lay out my clothes for dinner."

"I still have that lipstick—"

"Don't need it, but thanks anyway." María Luisa scooted out of the salón and into the front bathroom. She turned on the light but not the fan, loudly closed the door, and then opened it a hair's width to eavesdrop on Rebeca's end of the conversation. It wasn't a very sisterly thing to do, but they both did it so often that the invasion of privacy was merely a drop in the bucket of guilt she would carry around for acting on what she heard:

"What's up, girl? . . . *Mucho*, but I can't talk about it over the phone . . . Far from it, but I'll have to tell you later. The walls have big, fat ears . . . I know, I know. But you know how she is, and things are only going to get worse . . . I'll try, but I can't promise. Hey, before I forget it, thanks again for the pipas . . . Yeah, Ethan really loved them. He loves anything spicy. They're gone already . . . When did you make more? . . . Well, judging by the way he inhaled them, you shouldn't have any trouble selling them."

Rebeca coughed dryly again. "I might do that . . . No, I don't have a fever. It's just a little cough . . . I *know* I should have worn a jacket last night . . . Mamá told me, but, of course, I knew better. At least I looked good, though, right? I'll take some medicine before I go to bed . . . You're wicked."

Rebeca laughed huskily. "But no . . . Not anymore . . . I'll tell you the whole story later . . . You don't say . . . He was bleeding? . . . Badly? . . . Well, that's what happens. When you mess with the bull, sometimes you get the horns . . . I'd like to think he's learned his lesson . . . Somehow, I doubt it, too . . . No, there's really no reason for me to."

Rebeca cleared her throat. "Because what's done is done . . . Yeah, a glass of water might help. How about I call you later? . . . No, *I'll* call *you* . . . We'll see . . . I hope so, too."

Rebeca coughed again. "Gotta run. Talk to you soon . . . *Adiós.*"

"Damn it," María Luisa sighed, quietly but not silently shutting the door before Rebeca hung up the phone. She flushed clean water down the toilet and pretended to wash her hands.

"Your fat ass can come out now," Rebeca said with a knock as she skated past the door. *That should keep her busy for a while*, she thought, lilting back to her room.

María Luisa's eyes danced side to side as she faced the mirror. Dizzy with ideas, her mind wandered, but her ass stayed in the bathroom for several minutes.

19:20 h

Mozart's Twenty-Ninth Symphony soothed Marisa's waning moments with Thomas as they lounged at a nun-approved distance on her bed.

"I don't have to guess who composed this one," Thomas said, scanning the track list on the rear of *The Best of Mozart*, "but I wish these damn things weren't so hard to deal with." He flipped the jewel case over and pinched the edge opposite the hinge, though it was clear that the case was closed. He pinched it thirty more times, fifteen on the top corner, fifteen on the bottom one, and then rhythmically wiped the case clear of fingerprints with the bottom of the shirt.

Marisa reached over and coaxed the CD from him, tickling his bare stomach as she did so. "That's why I'm here," she said.

The sensation sent a chill through Thomas's body that made him laugh, although he didn't find her overture funny. "Hey, hands to yourself."

"*Culpa mía, Generalísimo,*" she saluted him with a laugh of her own. She rolled off the bed and stacked Mozart on top of Julio Iglesias, Mecano, Miguel Bosé, and Alex y Cristina.

Thomas shook his head. "Don't make me sorry I told you about that old fart at the church. You really are incorrigible."

"I know," she admitted from the foot of the bed, "but if I weren't, I couldn't ask you this: Whose are better, mine or hers?"

"Whose *what*?"

"*Tetas*," she whispered.

"How should I know?" he whispered back, struggling to look at her. The stack of CDs needed to be straightened and pushed back from the edge of the dresser.

"Well, you've seen hers."

"And?"

Marisa lifted her shirt and bra. A flash would have been exciting enough, but the pose lingered, her nipples tightening into small peas, like the gravel under the plane tree on the church grounds. "And now you've seen mine."

"Put your shirt down. Holy shit, I can't believe you just did that."

"Well, believe it," she said, making herself decent as she rolled back onto the bed. "So, whose are better? I want to know."

Thomas turned beet red as he scooted away from her.

"Well?"

"You're not going to let this go, are you?"

"Not until you answer me."

The images that were flashing through his mind would have broken her. The last thing he wanted to do was to hurt her feelings, so he told her just enough of the truth: "Yours are bigger."

"I know that, but whose are better?"

"That depends on what you mean by 'better.'"

"Ones that you would never get tired of touching."

"Well, when you put it that way . . ."

Marisa sat up, arching her back as she stretched. "Ones that would never get tired of your touch."

Thomas's face got even redder. "I don't think I would ever get tired of touching any breasts, big or small."

"Then mine are definitely better," Marisa declared.

"What makes you so sure?" he asked, inching still farther away.

She began to rub her nipples to soften them. "Because Lina won't let you touch hers, although you've been pining for her for God knows how long. What *exactly* has all that pining gotten you?"

The question nearly made him fall off the bed.

"Nowhere. Tell me I'm wrong."

He couldn't.

"But I'd let you touch mine and me anywhere you wanted, anytime you wanted. All you have to do is ask."

But I don't want to, he told himself with a profound sadness that for once was directed outward.

"All you have to do is ask," she repeated.

"I know, but, I've tried to tell you—"

"To keep my mouth shut."

Thomas nodded. "But you never seem to learn. Incorrigible. I told you."

Watching his attention shift from his wrist to the CDs and back again, Marisa wondered which one of them was more anguished. "You know this is about more than boobs, right?" she whispered. "I'm offering you a chance at a happier life."

Thomas was slow to respond. "You seem to think I deserve a chance like that."

"I don't *think* you do, I *know* you do."

"Well, I don't."

"Why the hell not?" she asked with a humph.

"Because . . ."

"Because why?"

"Because Lina—"

"Oh, screw Lina," Marisa insisted, choosing her words poorly, but she continued: "Why don't you deserve to be happy?"

As it had two nights ago, their conversation had taken an awkward turn. Tonight, Thomas had absolutely no doubt that he was listening to the genius of Mozart, or that he wanted to be nothing more than just the best of friends. He swallowed repeatedly, trying to clear the lump in his throat before changing the subject: "I need to run an errand tonight."

"Nice try, *guapo*. Answer my question."

He tugged four times at the bracelet around his wrist. "Because Lina has—"

"If that bitch had never been born, would you have the right to happiness?"

"You and I would never meet, have met if she had never been born."

"You're trying to dodge the question," Marisa said, taking him by the wrist, "but I'm not going to let you. You have OCD, that's all, and don't you have the same goddamn right to the 'pursuit of happiness,' to borrow a famous phrase, as everyone else?"

"Quoting Thomas Jefferson," Thomas said. "I'm impressed."

"Thank you, but what's your answer?"

"My answer is that *pursuing* happiness is a whole lot easier than *finding* it."

"You're twisting my words a bit."

"I don't mean to, but everything that goes on in my head gets a bit twisted."

Marisa could feel everything fading away—him, the hope of them, time. "Let's start with something more basic."

"Okay."

"Aren't you a good person?"

Thomas knew his answer before she had finished the question, but it took him a moment to say the word: "No."

"You can't really feel that way."

"Well, I do."

"Tell me why."

There was no hesitation this time: "Because of my OCD, I hurt people."

Marisa's fingers interlaced with his. "Hurt people? Oh, sweetie—"

"I don't want to, but it just happens."

"If you're talking about what I think you're talking about—"

"And I think I'm going to go back for that, that . . ."

"I'm happy to go with you. Let me get ready, and we'll go."

"But there's the problem of the money."

"I can probably give you some," she said as she rolled off the bed.

Thomas's hand slipped out of Marisa's. "You don't have it to give."

"No, but Mercedes does."

He shook his head. "I don't want to ask Mercedes for money."

"I'm talking about a small loan."

"Sending checks or money through the mail would be too complicated." His heart began to pound with anxiety at the thought of addressing an envelope, sealing it, putting a stamp on it, and putting it in the mailbox. He stood up.

Marisa touched him on the arm. "Silly, I meant that she could give *me* the money, and *I'd* pay her back."

He shook his head again. "I couldn't ask you to do that. Besides, then I'd owe you—"

"The money would be my gift to you. Anyway, you aren't asking. I'm offering." She gently patted his back pocket. "Wouldn't that be a way for you to get the money?"

A look of panicked desperation came over his face. "Oh, I already know how to get it."

20:30 h

Raindrops dotted the cobblestones of the Plaza de España as Ethan lingered in the antique shop's open doorway. He had no affection for the scent of rain, but it wafted into his nostrils, displacing the sweet aroma of *jazmín* he now associated with antiques. He had a tendency to link smells to occasions, places, and things. Though faded memories of this moment would never be more than a jasmine-scented candle away, what he was holding would never be far from his mind.

Of all his purchases this trip, none was as artistic and useful. It was only fitting that the saleswoman had placed it in the most beautiful paper sack he had ever seen, with branches of crayon-rubbed leaves set against a clear sky that was as blue as he was on nights like this one.

Lost in preoccupation, he crisped the folded top of the sack and rent its fibers into softening stubble between fingernails that were cut to the quick. The slivers of flesh had been in retreat for years and lost their painful sensitivity: a fringe benefit of anxious tendencies as he scraped through a coarse world. His loafers flirted with the threshold, but they dared not touch it.

A breeze tickled the wind chime overhead, its whimsical clinks heralding the resuscitation of breathless autumn skies. Panels frozen by a fresh coat of varnish popped and cracked as the door swelled with humidity. Outside, beyond the arcade, the fiestas waned.

A low-set fellow whose girth was testimony to his wares of thick chocolate and coils of fried dough cursed a well-traveled cart. The bullying rag crammed dowels of leather bracelets into a cosmetic case. Tapas crawlers hastened inside Café Sol, juggling glasses of reds and whites, and plates of stuffed olives and cubes of tortilla de patatas. Flitting sparrows thieved from abandoned baskets of bread.

Among empty hulls strewn about a bench lay a tube of pipas. Three pigeons were gorging themselves on the spillage; others quickly joined them. The white ones were Ethan's favorites. Las Rozas had just a few of them.

One, two.

The wind chime tinkled, fell silent, and then came to life, striking a dissonant chord that made Ethan wince. He pinched the fold as the sack blew against him. The euros tucked under his fingers fluttered.

Three.

A sparrow lit on the bench and began to feed on a thin heel of baguette bread. Peck by peck, the crusty bit crumbled toward the edge and fell onto the cobblestones, where it was snatched by a stout-bodied latecomer that limped off with it to the periphery.

Four.

Ethan's hand surrendered the paper edge with a twitch, and the corners of his mouth curved slightly upward in an archaic smile. He placed the sack in his palm. The paper crinkled as it flattened under the weight of the small box inside, and he lightly closed his fingertips around it. *There's room in the carry-on for this.*

He stared at the dusky sky framed by the arch a few meters in front of him. Ragged clouds floated on the town's misty glow. Wispy tatters of gray and purple seemed to tiptoe along the ridge of the roof across the square. *Six months of hell and six months of winter*, he thought, inverting the proverb about weather on the Meseta. *The transition's finally begun. I wonder if Satan's bath will delay the flight.*

Ethan's chest rose as he finished the bittersweet thought. A shallow sigh belied his profound anxiety. His eyes fell, their brightness fading to a bleary reflection of the shuttered windows below the distant roof. The open louvers bathed the façade with a warmth suggestive of the ardent conversations that had recently taken place nearby.

A stirring gust ruffled the euros again. The flutter evoked

memories of Rebeca's and María Luisa's playful ribbing about the coins that often lay neglectedly in his pocket. But he had done better this time. Fishing around in his change pocket, he had come up a few céntimos short. Flustered, he had been tempted to spend the small bill in the other pocket, but experience had taught him better, and he had resisted. Diffidence didn't lend itself to bargaining, so he had broken his last large bill, reluctantly. *Damn value-added tax. I'm not even a resident of the European Union—*

The rag had finished his packing and was at it again. This time his quarry was a middle-aged man, whose response to the bully's sales pitch was a curt rejection before hurrying off toward Café Sol without a whiff of intimidation.

Ethan watched the rag slink toward the gazebo. *No not-so-veiled threat, no stinging funny bone, no parting slur. I'm a freakin' human doormat,* he told himself yet again, *but you're not getting another chance to wipe your ratty sneakers on me. And I still don't want to see the clean edge your new blade leaves.* Ethan slid out of sight.

Behind the display window, he tucked the sack under his arm and set about organizing his money. He arranged the bills from smallest to largest, obverses up and facing the same direction, of course, and doubled them twice. From his back pocket he withdrew his makeshift wallet, poked the euros inside, and nudged them and his credit card toward the bottom. He slipped the packet back into its pocket and felt for the slit in the flap that had been undone since his purchase.

¡Hostias!

That the button came off wasn't really a surprise. Ethan had never been comfortable in new clothing: It seemed to wear him. He bought most of his pants and shirts at a secondhand store, his meticulous nature well suited to finding spotless bargains among the discards. As it was with the crinkled spine of a used book, loose buttons were just part of the deal, and he could manage with needle and thread. But since his mother's death he had found little time for mending.

In an ironic gesture, he pinched the tiny disk between his thumb and forefinger and wedged his hand into his pocket to nudge the folded paper toward the bottom.

He was an easy mark and had been approached several times on the streets of Madrid, his impeccable accent and ample vocabulary a handy defense. In Las Rozas he still felt safe, but during the fiestas even Álvaro was cautious; the nudge became a push, the push a shove, the paper sticking to his fingers. *The bills really fattened it up. It looks too much like a wallet now to keep it in front, and I'm not putting it in my sock.*

Ethan eased his hand out of his pocket and plucked the tag of khaki thread, rolling it into an afterthought before laying it and the button on the display counter in front of him, careful not to smudge the glass, which smelled lightly of vinegar. Letting his eyelids fall, he inhaled deeply, held it, and then exhaled before opening his eyes.

He paid more attention to fasteners than most men, and it had been his experience that two-hole buttons were far less reliable than those with four holes, setting aside the weight of the thread used to attach them. Two-hole buttons, however, he found much more interesting: a Rorschach test of sorts. Staring at the disk that lay before him, he saw the bald head of a man with a long, flat nose and pursed lips, and then the face of a barn owl whose large pupils reflected a birder's spotlight.

It was stupid of me not to have checked this, Ethan chided himself. He placed his fingertip on the button. The plastic stuck to his finger as he slid the disk toward him. After a tantalizing tap against the trim along the front of the counter, he coaxed the button onto the metal strip, and then took the sack from under his wing and placed it on the glass. Backlit by a microfluorescent tube, the silhouette inside the thin paper gave him pause. He thought of his mother as he pulled the sweater down over his pocket. *It's long enough—*

"You're welcome to borrow my sewing kit."

Ethan turned to look at the saleswoman who had just come out of the back. She was carrying a small box.

"I would do it myself," she said, "but it's in an awkward place."

"Thank you," he said, collecting himself. "My sweater's long enough to cover it."

"You have to be careful of pickpockets," she urged. "They're bad during the fiestas, especially for an American."

"My sweater's probably long enough."

"I would hate to see you lose something important."

The thought of losing anything at all made Ethan's heart race, but he resisted. "I'll be careful. I always am. Besides, this isn't exactly the place to re-attach a button."

"Of course not, but there's a bathroom in back. It's all yours."

"I *am* quite the seamster," Ethan joked. "Thank you very much, but I think I'll wait until I have the time to do it right."

The saleswoman smiled. "It would only take a second."

"I have a dinner at nine o'clock," he said with a quick check of the clocks on the wall.

"How about a needle and some thread to take with you, then? I'm sure I have the right color," she added, opening the box.

"You're very kind, but I'm leaving first thing in the morning." The words tripped off Ethan's tongue.

"That's a shame."

Although she was trying to be helpful, the last thing Ethan needed was another conversation about tomorrow. He slid the button off the counter and coaxed his fist into his pocket. "I'll put it in here for later," he said and glanced over his shoulder out the window. Through squinted eyes he could make out the fountain. There was no one there.

"Very well."

"It doesn't look like María Luisa has finished her shopping . . . or whatever she's doing. Would you mind if I waited inside a little longer?"

"I had thought about closing early, but take as long as you need," the saleswoman said with a wink.

"Thank you."

"Don't mention it." She placed the kit beside the register. "I'll leave this here in case you change your mind."

"I don't think I will, but thank you again for everything."

"You're quite welcome, and if you'll excuse me, I need to make a phone call in back."

"Of course."

"Hurry back," she added, parting the curtain, but before stepping into the back of the shop, she paused. "And do be careful."

"I'll try," he said with a tug on his sweater. "I will."

"Someone who looks closely will see it, too." She winked again and then slipped out of sight.

Ethan flushed as the curtain closed behind her.

20:45 h

Ethan's stomach growled as he slouched behind the shop's display window, his mind too preoccupied to remind him to stand up straight.

The rain clouds had done little more than connect the dots on the cobblestones, so the weather wasn't what was keeping María Luisa, if she was even late. Spaniards weren't known for their punctuality, and Spain's internal clock ran accordingly. He had learned that lesson his first night as an exchange student—another "difference." He poked at the tiny hole in his pocket, staring.

There was a vacancy to his gaze, as if he were oblivious to those who paused to window-shop, but he was simply ignoring them, looking through them like a camera set on infinity. Beyond the cobblestones, traffic on Avenida Toreros was light. A handful of pigeons were foraging inside the fountain, their pale gray heads bobbing into and out of view as they searched the damp litter for pipas.

Perched on the shoulder of the Virgen de la Retamosa like an albino parrot, one of Ethan's favorites groomed itself with oil from the gland at the base of its tail. The bird's contortions were predictable as it tidied up each feather. When it stuck its tail in the statue's ear, Ethan wondered what the appropriate penance was for giving a stone virgin a wet willy. *Forgive him Father for he has sinned.*

Confessing on the bird's behalf made Ethan chuckle. Pigeons were incapable of sin, as were all birds and wild creatures. He had always believed that all animals, save one, went straight to Heaven when they died. That one exception, of course, was modern man. Plagued with a conscience, the most dangerous member of the animal kingdom was rife with sin.

Ethan tried not to dwell on death. What would happen when he died was a question to which science provided only theoretical answers and to which faith afforded only convictions, not truths. More often than not, he believed there was an afterlife and that he would escape everlasting punishment. Whether his blessed self jetted directly to paradise or laid over briefly in a state of torment to make amends before flying on, he hoped to land in his version of Heaven—a small house warmed by love and embraced by woods and mountains.

Ethan watched the rag pitch another "customer." The bully's tone was insistent and obnoxious, but he was quickly rebuffed and let his quarry go: no threat, no grab, no slur. Ethan gave a sigh of self-reproach and let his imagination wander to that small house in the woods . . .

The cabin was livable, above all else, and the perfect size for the two of them—two, not three. It was cozy and tastefully decorated with rock-and-mineral décor throughout the first-floor great room and second-floor master bedroom loft. Its rustic charm was exceeded only by its views of the night sky from a wraparound porch with two rocking chairs, although they hadn't aged a day since they first met.

Their dogs were also young again, free from the ills of old age his selfishness had made them suffer. They spent their days romping to their hearts' content in the woods and their nights running in their sleep on a thick rug in front of the fireplace.

Occasionally, the two of them left the dogs at home and ventured out alone. They strolled barefoot along mossy paths in deep forests, around clear lakes, and through glades of white and purple wildflowers. They scrambled over boulders and explored shallow, gravel-bed streams, counting the flecks of golden mica and specks of red garnet in each handful.

Her adventure wear was casual and flirty (rolled-up jeans, versatile scarf, and a light-colored tank top), but when the cool water tightened her nipples, she became downright sexy. And she hardly knew it. It was one of the things he loved about her. When she slipped her bra off without taking off her shirt, splashed water down the front of her, and commanded him to "bring those lips over here," the rush of the stream paled in comparison to the rush of emotions—

But even Ethan's daydream was haunted by that despicable voice. Its relentless demands pinched him awake as they grew louder. His pulse quickened, and as he cupped the bulge in his back pocket, his eyes came into focus. Even with the display window's wavy glass, there was no mistaking the face. It was only a matter of time until he was helpless against it, like an actor with stage fright wishing away a bout of hiccups.

He wrested the hand from his pocket, grabbed the sack with an about-face, did the last buttons on his sweater, and shuffled toward the doorway.

"Money," the voice demanded again. The tone was desperate.

He curled the crisped fold into his fist and inched forward. The rag's back was toward him. *Now or never*, he told himself, and with a tap of the foot he decided to go.

Leaving was a hasty yet positive affront to the uneasiness that continued to nag at him. With the gait of legs twisted in the womb, his toe caught on the threshold. He stumbled into the arcade with an inopportune thud, his right hand pressed against the cobbles, his left extended out and behind, crouching like a sprinter at the start.

"Boy!"

Embarrassment was the least of his concerns. He rose quickly, wiped the grit off his hand, and yanked the sweater down over his pocket before starting up the passageway. His head swiveled toward the plaza, behind him, and then back, searching as the tips of his fingers skimmed the granite arches.

The igneous rock felt like sandpaper. The image of his Geology 101 classroom flashed into his mind. Minerals and the "Scale of Scratchability" couldn't help him now.

The memory and the arches passed quickly, and he paused under the lantern that hung at the end of the arcade. There was a tiny hole in the sack.

"Boy!"

He tugged impotently on his sweater. Still no sign of María Luisa. *The bus stop will do, but down the back, the long way.* Another about-face, but in the pale light he could see that the steps were wet. The awning that he remembered was gone, and each narrow tread glistened more than the one above it. With well-worn loafers he wondered if the handrail would be enough. And then there was the hike up Maestro Alonso, or rather Calle Maestro Alonso: Spaniards rarely omit the word for "street." *I should have gotten those half soles.*

There was that word again—"should"—but the self-rebuke would have to wait. He spun back, doubtful that the short walk across the plaza would help. *I may have to go looking for her*, he thought and cast an anxious glance over his shoulder. "Promise or not—"

The saleswoman was talking to someone, gesticulating with a

cordless telephone in the doorway, tapping her foot on the sagging timber that had sent him reeling. What she was saying or to whom he could not tell.

He scooted under the keystone and quickly fixed his sock. The arch's thick pier partly obscured his view of the arcade, but the conversation had attracted the attention of the fishmonger, who was standing in his doorway, cleaning a fillet knife on his bloody apron.

"Yuck," Ethan whispered, fixing his sock again, and then caught the cowled face of a *rape*, monkfish, among the raw fish and shellfish on ice in the monger's display window: *Lord, monkfish are ugly*. He narrowed his eyes and began to name the other ones that hadn't gotten away: *goose barnacles, crayfish, octopus, lobster, spiny lobster—*

Discordant clanks halted the review as the saleswoman took the purse strap off her shoulder and slipped it over her head. As she reached to silence the wind chime, light from the shop gave a hint of something in her hand. She inched backward, her gesticulations with the handset subdued, and then buttoned her raincoat still holding what he could now see was a familiar box. *The sewing kit . . . the thread.*

Mystery solved.

"Boy!"

The anxiety was acute.

The saleswoman pointed the antenna up the arcade and spoke. The monger chimed in with a gristly voice.

From where Ethan stood, the monger's words were nearly unintelligible, but he heard him say, "*Guardia Civil.*"

The sack grazed the pier as he backpedaled onto the plaza.

Tasty, though, he remembered as his thoughts turned from the monkfish to his mother. She hated fish.

20:56 h

Ethan parted the tattered fliers taped to the back of the bus stop shelter and ran his finger down the HORARIO DE AUTOBUSES—FIESTAS.

"20:58 h," he mouthed: "8:58 p.m." Converting twenty-four-hour time to twelve-hour time was second nature to him.

He had stopped wearing a watch when his mother died. But since there was no sign of the bus, which usually ran on schedule at that time of day, he supposed they wouldn't be too late to savor a plate of his favorite patatas before what was sure to be an especially boisterous Spanish dinner began.

Across the plaza, long shadows danced among the umbrella tables of Café Sol at the end of the west arcade, but shops were going dark on both sides of the square. Perhaps María Luisa was just being Spanish. He mashed the small bill in his pocket, conforming the damp paper to his pocket knife, and dug the slippery sole of one loafer and then the other into the edge of the bench as he fixed his socks.

Cigarette butts, pipas hulls, puffed cornmeal *gusanitos*, and trampled shreds of eye-catching handbills for last night's concert littered the stop. Promotional carpet bombing. To hell with the trees.

Mementos came in all shapes and sizes, including ragged rectangles, one of which was wedged in the trim along the bottom of the shelter. He stooped to pluck what could have been an addition to his next photo album, unaware that his sweater had dragged open the flap on his buttonless pocket. The scrap came free without tearing, and he tilted it toward a streetlight.

Although it had succeeded in catching his attention, the fluorescent green paper made the artsy print difficult to read, but he immediately recognized the band's name: "The Princeton Pedants," he said softly. Translating English to Spanish was also second nature to him: "*Los Pedantes de Princeton*." He whispered the names to himself over and over, loving the witty oxymoron and the alliteration and remembering hips swaying to the fusion of pop and classical guitar.

The CD had cost him ten euros (about thirteen dollars), more than he could really spend on indulgences so late into the trip. But the staccato chords alone would trigger priceless memories and keep the fire burning. He was like his mom when it came to those kinds of things; a fat bank account would not have saved her anyway.

The bus's pneumatic brakes screeched in the distance. But he was lost in the scrap, oblivious to his surroundings, even his white pigeons, until a resurgent uneasiness jostled him like a twilight reveille.

After a quick debate, he undid the sack's once crisp fold and let go of the shred, resisting the urge to watch it fall. He closed the sack and began to run his finger along the fold as he peered over the fliers, looking through his reflection as he searched for his birds.

One, two.

But Ethan wasn't alone.

"The money . . ."

And he hadn't been alone for quite a while.

"Boy!"

Raindrops tapped on the bus stop. Its transparent walls had been no shelter at all.

Ethan stepped back as he reached for his back pocket. "No, I'm not giving you what you want. I said no," he insisted, tucking the sack under his arm.

"The credit card."

"Leave me the hell alone," Ethan begged and shoved his hand into his front pocket.

"All of it."

He clenched the Swiss army knife and backpedaled onto the painted curb as he glanced toward the fountain. "Mar—"

Startled by the hissing squeal of brakes, he tumbled backward into the street and was hit by the bus.

MONDAY, 7 OCTOBER 2002

Las Rozas, Spain

02:10 h

A claustrophobic fog clung to Avenida de la Constitución. The Iglesia de San Miguel was a ghost of itself. The scarlet of the nave doors was turned a misty garnet. The glow from the pair of sconces was scattered into haloes.

Ethan's window and shutter were open. Moist with dew, the edge of the sill dug into Rebeca's fingers as she stood there, staring outside, trying to make sense of anything. "Fly to the angels," she whispered.

Even with the light spilling out of the salón, the bedroom was dark enough for Rebeca to have curled up on the bed and fallen asleep. But not even the sweetest dream would have been as sweet as what had been lost. This was the stuff of nightmares, as it was for María Luisa, whose shadow stretched into the room before she found the strength to enter. "Can't sleep?" she asked, cinching her robe.

Rebeca shook her head.

The soles of María Luisa's slippers squeaked across the floor. "Me neither," she said, resting her chin on Rebeca's shoulder as she gave her the hug she hadn't gotten in years. "This room is cursed."

For a few moments the two sisters were one. Words escaped both of them, or at least the right ones, but not even death could bring them together for long. "He was fine," Rebeca said faintly. "After he regained consciousness, he was perfectly fine. Talking, making sense. His mind was clear. I don't understand."

"Didn't the doctor explain the lucid interval to you?" María Luisa asked gently.

"Yes, but you said the bus didn't hit him."

"It didn't. He fell into it."

"And when he did . . ." Rebeca's words faded.

María Luisa took a deep breath and finished the thought her

sister couldn't: "His brain got . . . mushed up against his skull, and it started to bleed. After a while, his body couldn't take it."

Rebeca began to resist María Luisa's embrace. "I should have been there."

"You *were* there," she said, squeezing her tighter. "We both were until they rushed us out of the room when he started to crash."

"Not the hospital. I meant the bus stop," Rebeca said, her voice breaking.

"There was nothing you could have done."

"Then help me understand what happened because it doesn't make sense."

"None of it does," María Luisa said, letting her go, "but I'll try." She backpedaled toward the bed, carefully parted Ethan's belongings, and sat down.

Rebeca went to cross herself, but stopped, and then turned her back to the outside world. "You were going to meet at the fountain."

María Luisa nodded.

"And he said that even though Mamá's friend wanted to close up early, he was welcome to stay."

"That's what he said."

"So why was he at the bus stop?"

"You know him, knew him," María Luisa said, struggling with the right tense, "he wouldn't have wanted to inconvenience her."

"But she said he could stay." Rebeca blotted her eyes with her sleeve.

María Luisa nodded again.

"Was someone bothering him?"

The question had no good answer. "I didn't see anyone."

"Could you see things clearly enough to know for sure?"

Again, no good answer, so María Luisa just sighed.

"What did you see happen, then?"

"I saw him back out of the bus stop, holding what he had bought—"

"He couldn't stop talking about how beautiful it was. The sack, too."

"Where is that—"

"I can still hear him shouting my name," María Luisa interrupted.

"When did he shout your name?"

"Right before he slipped. I can still see him falling, but in slow motion. He banged into the bus and just collapsed. There was nothing I could do."

Rebeca's eyes filled again with tears. "Why weren't you with him?" she whimpered.

"I should have been, but I just wasn't."

"Why not?"

Rebeca's question was more mournful than accusatory, but her sister answered it anyway. "It took me longer to track down Paloma than—"

"Paloma?"

María Luisa's eyes dropped to the floor.

"Why were you looking for Paloma?"

"Because I wanted to buy—"

"Pipas," Rebeca said, blotting her eyes again.

"Yes."

"I *knew* you were listening to my conversation."

"I was. But you do the same thing."

Rebeca took a deep breath as she nodded. "I do, but if you hadn't been snooping, he would still be alive."

María Luisa put her hand on his suitcase. "You're not telling me anything I haven't told myself a thousand—"

"We'll never know," Sra. Navas said, silhouetted in the doorway. "If there's one thing I know, life's full of questions that don't have answers." She reached for the light switch, but decided the light would be much too painful. "You two should try to get some sleep."

"*Imposible*," Rebeca said as her mother's embrace swallowed María Luisa, whose hand never left the suitcase.

Then Sra. Navas embraced her younger daughter. "Do me a favor and at least try," Sra. Navas whispered into her ear. "And you need another dose of medicine."

Rebeca disagreed with a look of profound sadness.

"You've been standing in front of that window and breathing in the night air."

"Mamá, I don't need it."

"How about a cup of chamomile tea, then?"

"Not right now."

"María Luisa?"

"Maybe later," she said, her spirits falling.

"Well, today's going to be a difficult day, but somehow we'll get through it," Sra. Navas said, choking up as she glanced outside. "What choice do we have?" She kissed each daughter goodnight. "Knock if you need anything."

"I will," Rebeca said and let go of her mother's hand.

María Luisa nodded repeatedly.

"Good night, my *two* dears," Sra. Navas said softly, with a pat for each of them. And then the woman who had lost another son shuffled out the door.

"*Buenas noches, Mamá,*" her daughters said in unison.

02:25 h

As a child, María Luisa's head used to swim with creative ways to reuse everyday objects: Newspapers were reborn as wrapping paper, wine corks were sliced and glued into coasters, T-shirts were sewn and stuffed into pillows. But grownup disillusion had bruised her creativity. And now, shock and grief had crushed it altogether. Instead of imagining the empty tissue box in her hand as a frilly piggy bank or a sequined jewelry box, she saw nothing but a worthless, hollow cube, which she blankly set aside before drowning another Kleenex in the toilet. She wasn't one to leave empty boxes and rolls for the next person, unless that person was Rebeca, but tonight the last thing on her mind was attending to trivialities.

There was nothing trivial about his dying instruction: "Take care of it for me."

"It" was the small box inside a paper sack that evoked the mental landscape he had once painted for her of autumn in his corner of Virginia. She would love to have seen those ancient mountains and rolling foothills ablaze with brilliant reds, golden yellows, and vibrant oranges. But that sky-blue dream likely died with him, and now she had to face the possibility that, like his brain, his beautiful purchase hadn't survived the impact.

Fearing his fragile state, she had told him that "it was unharmed," although she hadn't even opened the sack. It was one of those necessary lies you never confess to telling if it turns out to be true or for which later you are easily forgiven if it doesn't.

Whichever the case, the courage to peek inside the sack, which now lay neatly on her dresser, was eluding her. Or maybe it wasn't the looking but the touching of the embodiment of a dysfunction that was provoking so much heartbreaking anxiety.

She took four cleansing breaths, rocked the light switch off, and opened the bathroom door. Counting the squeaks of her slippers, she wandered back toward her room. Rebeca's light was on, as was the one in her parents' room. Their door was closed, as María Luisa's should have been. Her pace quickened.

Entering the room, she found Rebeca sitting on the side of the bed. Ethan's microcassette recorder lay on the flattened sack beside her, and in her quivering hands the open box cast a pall over the already dim cloister. "What the hell are you doing?" María Luisa shouted.

"I just wanted to see."

"And now you have, so put it away."

Rebeca just sat there.

"Put it away," she shouted again. "It's not yours, and neither is *that*." María Luisa reached for the recorder, but was rebuffed. "How dare you get into his suitcase."

"And how dare *you* keep this for yourself?" Rebeca snapped back, closing the box.

"I'm not keeping it; he asked *me* to take care of it, and that's what I'm doing. And for now, I've decided it's staying right here."

"It belongs to—"

"And I'm sure you've listened to the tape, too," María Luisa accused, her loud voice trembling.

"I haven't had the heart," Rebeca whispered.

"Well, thank God for small miracles—"

"God has nothing to do with any of this," Sra. Navas interrupted. "You two are *really* something else. Do you know how ridiculous you sound arguing at a time like this?"

Neither daughter said a word.

"And I don't have to ask what you're arguing about because Papá and I could hear you through the wall. *Por Dios*, Álvaro's grandmother could probably hear you from upstairs." Sra. Navas shuffled toward the bed. "This is over."

María Luisa bristled. "It's not over—"

"I said it's over."

"It's not over until she minds her own business."

"What has she—"

"She's invaded his privacy, and now she needs to put back what isn't hers."

Sra. Navas slid the sack out from under the recorder and reached to take the box from Rebeca, who surrendered it after a final peek inside. Sra. Navas returned it to the sack, which she placed in María Luisa's eager palm. "He handed this to you, so it's yours to look after until his father arrives."

"What about the recorder?"

"What about it?"

"She should have to put it back exactly where she found it."

"Where did you—"

"In his suitcase," María Luisa said, cutting off her mother. "And *she* shouldn't be allowed to listen to the message from *his* mother anyway."

"Have you already listened to it?"Sra. Navas asked.

Rebeca shook her head. "But he told me I could."

"When did he tell you that?" her sister asked loudly, taking offense.

"In the hospital."

"I didn't hear him say that."

"You, Mamá, and Papá had stepped out of the room to talk to the nurse, so I guess you don't know everything, do you?"

"Shut—"

"That is yours to take care of, then," Sra. Navas told Rebeca, gesturing toward the recorder. "And whether to listen to the message or not is up to you."

María Luisa pouted.

"Tranquila, hija."

"How can that be your decision?"

"Because I absolutely believe her."

María Luisa angrily re-cinched her robe. "Well, I don't."

"And because it's only fair that each of you has something of his to look after," Sra. Navas added.

"But it's a private message. Obviously, she's going to listen to it. She can't help herself."

Sra. Navas wiped the tear from her daughter's cheek. "Could *you*, my dear?"

"I could if that is what he wanted," María Luisa said, incredulously lauding her self-restraint.

"*¡Una mierda!*—Like hell!" Rebeca coughed. "You're so full of shit."

A smile of annoyed amusement formed on Sra. Navas's mouth. She gave each of her daughters a knowing look.

María Luisa shot Rebeca a look of her own, and then admitted to her mother what she already knew: "Maybe not."

"That's what I thought," Sra. Navas said. "My decision is final, *¿entendido?*"

Her daughters halfheartedly agreed, and the three women lingered in silence. For how long, God only knew, and Sra. Navas saw no point in asking him that or any other question. She hugged and kissed each daughter goodnight again, but instead of leaving, she went and closed the door.

"When you become a mother," she said, "you quickly realize that children are a blessing and a curse. But mostly a blessing. From the moment they pop out of you, if you're lucky, you begin to love them more than life itself and to worry about them every moment of every day. You would do anything to protect them." Her voice started to fade. "In that regard, I guess I have failed as a mother because two of my children—I say two, although only *one* was actually mine—are gone."

"It's okay, Mamá," Rebeca managed to say.

Reluctantly, María Luisa sat down on the end of the bed. "Take as long as you need," she whispered, tasting a salty tear as she fussed with her robe. She leaned her charge against her hip and wiped her eyes. For a moment, the sack and the recorder were inches apart, but the woman who had told her daughters to look after them suspected that at any moment a powder keg could blow the rift between them wide open.

Sra. Navas forced herself to continue: "My instinct is to protect all of my children from pain, and lately it's been hard to hover on the periphery, watching and listening without interjecting myself into your decisions. I've had my preferences, of course, but I've still given you plenty of latitude, whether you realize it or not. What happens now is also up to you."

Rebeca placed the recorder in her lap. "If you're worried about our behavior when his father comes to collect—"

"In trying times, what's better left unsaid often isn't."

"We would never argue in front of his father," María Luisa promised, cupping the sack.

Blotting her eyes, Rebeca nodded in agreement.

"I'm sure you wouldn't do it intentionally, but at any moment, either of you is likely to blurt out something that you can never take back. Find it within yourselves to love each other, to cherish your memories and your private moments, and above all else, to hold your tongues. Nothing good will come of it if you don't."

"But when good things happen to bad people," Rebeca said, "I want to scream."

"But you don't need to do it at your sister; talk to me instead. Your anger . . . and your secrets . . . and your questions are safe with me. The same goes for both of you."

"Some questions are harder than others," María Luisa said.

"You can ask me anything."

"So why *does* God allow bad things to happen to good people?" Rebeca asked.

"Interesting question."

"And please don't say that we're not supposed to ask such questions," Rebeca continued, choking up. "I can't take an answer like that."

Sra. Navas sighed. "Me neither, but that's the answer I've gotten more times than I can count since I was barely a tadpole. I promise to do better than *my* mother did."

"Please. So?"

"So I've had my answer to that question since not long after Félix died. At the time, I thought that my precious baby was taken from me, that God had called him home because he had special plans for him."

"And now?" María Luisa asked, clutching the sack to her chest.

"Now Félix lives in my memory and in my heart. *They* are his home."

Rebeca shifted. "But don't you read in the Bible that—"

"Oh, my dear, I stopped reading that book years ago."

Her daughters exchanged quizzical glances.

"Historical romances are my thing. I read at least one paperback a week, and then I donate it to the church."

"You shut yourself in your room to read romance novels?" Rebeca asked.

"That's right."

"But I've seen you sitting with the Bible in your lap," María Luisa insisted.

"It's a prayer book, not the Bible, and I keep it beside me on the bed so I can switch the two when you knock."

Rebeca shifted again, her palms sticking to the recorder. "That's being dishonest."

"No, that's being a coward. And a slave to . . ."

"A slave to what?" María Luisa prodded.

"To keeping up appearances."

"Keeping up appearances?" Rebeca asked. "I'm not sure I understand. I don't care if you read romance novels. Read away. You don't need to be embarrassed about—"

"I'm not embarrassed."

"You might have to say a few Hail Marys for reading such racy stuff, but we all have our guilty pleasures."

"Pleasure, yes. Guilt, no," Sra. Navas confessed.

"Now, I really don't understand."

"But I think I'm beginning to," María Luisa whispered, her disillusionment deepening. "Mamá?"

"Yes, dear."

"What else have you been keeping from us? From me? You must have twisted a few tales in the name of 'keeping up appearances,' or am I wrong?"

"I'm much too tired to go into all of that right now," Sra. Navas said, dodging. "But even if I weren't, this would be a good time for you to accept that it's better to leave some things unsaid."

María Luisa shook her head. "I can't accept that answer, God knows."

"I told you that God has nothing to do with any of this," her mother said.

"And?"

"And what you believe is up to you."

The taste of salt was on María Luisa's lips again. "And what do you believe, Mamá?"

The answer sprang into Sra. Navas's mind, but it lingered on her tongue. "I believe . . ."

María Luisa leaned forward. "You believe . . ."

"I believe that my two boys are together now."

"In Heaven?" Rebeca managed to ask.

"Oh, my dear, that question can only be answered by faith."

Rebeca nodded. "But since you go to church every Sunday, you must have an answer."

"Going to church and believing are two very different things," her mother said, sliding up to the bed and pulling her girls toward her. "One is about being seen; the other is about not needing to see. As for me, tonight I see two beautiful, young women and one old lady. And if I were *un superman*, I could look through the wall and see one stubborn, old man tossing and turning under the covers. And just a little while ago I saw suitcases lying on a neatly made bed that replaced the empty crib I used to stare at for hours. But nowhere in the room that once held the promise of so much life, or in any other room in any other building in Spain, or in any granite block of any magnificent *acueducto* and *catedral*, or in any corner of the sky above them, did I ever set eyes on the invisible man who created all of it."

"That's why we have faith, Mamá."

"Not me, not anymore," Sra. Navas whispered, squeezing them tightly before letting them go. "Tell your father if you must, but when you share a bed with someone for as long as I have, it's hard to keep most secrets." After a glance at her daughters' charges, she crossed the room and grabbed the doorknob. "Most, but not all of her secrets. A woman's got to be allowed to have a few," she said with a wink and opened the door.

03:30 h

Rebeca's unwound alarm clock was frozen at a hair past two o'clock, not a.m. or p.m., just two o'clock. *What a difference twelve little hours make*, she thought, staring again at the nearly full bottle of cough syrup next to the microcassette recorder lying on the nightstand.

No one may have ever missed a cough more.

Weeping, she eased open the drawer, unplugged the headphones from her *walkman*, and plugged them into the recorder. *I can do this*, she tried to convince herself, tucking her hair behind her ears as she put on the headphones. She took a deep breath, pulled the covers up under her chin, and pressed PLAY.

After a few seconds of white noise in only one ear, the message began:

"Dear Ethan," said the pleasant voice that Rebeca had only heard over the telephone.

04:45 h

María Luisa had been up all night. If she had wandered back to the front bedroom, she would have seen that nothing had changed about the misty view out the window or the emptiness in the room where she had left Rebeca standing in the dark.

Come morning light, the "children" had planned to rise and shine, enjoy a leisurely breakfast, throw on some clothes, and head for the airport. Driving in heavy traffic in the rain had always made María Luisa nervous, but now there was no need to finesse the family car out of the garage and brave the cluttered A-6 superhighway. For that one, little thing she was thankful. Otherwise, she saw no reason to get out of bed, eat, get dressed, or step foot outside.

She had forced herself to return the sack to the dresser. In its top drawer was the small tube of spicy pipas she had bought from Paloma. The snack was likely to linger for eternity among her socks, bras, and panties. As María Luisa lay in bed, beating herself up over dawdling back to the fountain instead of hurrying to meet Ethan, there was a knock on her door.

"It's me," Rebeca whispered.

"What do you want?" María Luisa asked after making her wait.

"I need to talk to you for a moment."

She propped herself up on one elbow. "About what?"

"I'll be in my room," Rebeca said and tiptoed away.

María Luisa sat up. "Leave me alone," she begged, but there was no response. "Rebeca?" Still nothing. "Rebeca!" She threw herself back onto the pillow. *¡Uy, qué coñazo!* she screamed inwardly with every intention of ignoring the pain in the ass. But she couldn't and sat up again. *She'll just knock again, so I might as well try to make Mamá happy.*

Moments later, she slipped barefoot into Rebeca's room and pushed the door closed. "What do you want?"

Rebeca patted the bed. "Come sit down."

"You're exhausting."

"Come. Sit down."

Obliging after a moment's hesitation, María Luisa sank into the end of the bed. "No more shit tonight. I can't take it."

"No more shit, I promise." Rebeca reached into the nightstand. "Here, have a listen." Holding the recorder, she offered her the headphones. "It doesn't play in both ears, but you can still hear it fine."

Her sister was caught off guard. "It must be in mono, then."

"Must be," Rebeca said, repeating the offer. "Let me know if it's too loud."

"You know you don't have to do this."

"I know."

María Luisa spread the headphones and adjusted them to her ears. "Then why are you?"

"Because it's the right thing to do," Rebeca said. "It takes a moment for it to come on. Ready?"

"I'm not sure."

"Neither was I, but here goes anyway. Let me know when it gets to the end." She started the tape.

María Luisa's pulse pounded in her ears over the meaningless background noise, and then the message began:

"Dear Ethan, I was going to send you this letter, but your Aunt Deidre convinced me to read it into a tape recorder so you'd never forget the sound of my voice. I'm not sure my sister's right, but I didn't see the point of arguing about something that trivial, so here goes: Again, Dear Ethan, Letter writing is a dying art form, but I haven't forgotten everything the nuns taught me. So I thought I'd give it a go and begin by telling you that the weekend before the doctors found this thing that's going to kill me, I went fishing with your guide friend, Mark. Apparently, the cold spring had delayed the spawn, and the stripers were still way up the lake. What a long boat ride.

We pulled planer boards around the island where you caught your trophy fish. Mark still talks about how excited you were that day. I can't remember how many hits we got, but I only caught two. Mark said we might have done better if he could have caught smaller bait. I guess he threw the net for hours 'under them lights by Webster's.' (I think he meant Webster's Marina.) I had a blast anyway. The world needs more folks like Mark.

My new neighbors will take some getting used to. I can hear the kids running up and down the steps at all hours of the night. Don't the little darlings ever sleep? And they leave their bikes behind my car. I think they've even scratched it. I can't say anything to them, of course. Good luck selling my place after I'm gone.

Your dad and I rarely speak anymore, but I guess I can understand why. No, I take that back. I can't see why we can't be friends just because I couldn't stay married to him. I almost hate calling him with questions about my taxes and those sorts of things. There's always a tone in his voice.

I wish Grandpa Clemens lived closer. I miss seeing him. Your Grandma Clemens and I will never get along, however, but I still call them whenever I'm in town to see if I can drop by for a visit. Her attitude has gotten worse since the divorce, not that it was good before it. Have I ever told you that before your father and I got married, she told me I wasn't good enough for him? I guess I just did. Isn't it amazing how a woman who has never had a job in the real world can fault someone who has? I don't say a word.

I talk to your other grandmother every single day. Mom's her usual hypochondriacal self. Lately, she's started to trick the lady who cleans the house into taking her to the pharmacy. When she gets there, she suddenly remembers that she has toothpaste, toilet paper, or whatever, and goes to check her blood pressure. And if it's not her blood pressure, it's her bladder, her leg, a supposed brain tumor—that one's not funny anymore—or some other nonsense. I say the problem is that she has it too good, living with your aunt and uncle.

No one's going to take care of *me* like that when I get older. I was going to take care of it myself, if you know what I mean, but I guess I can stop looking for a cliff. She won't listen to reason, and our two-hour conversations wear me out. Daughters need to talk to their mothers more than sons do. I guess it's a woman thing.

But the reason for this letter is not to bore you with the details of my lonely life, but to tell you that I might not beat this thing. Glioblastomas are bad news, and I wouldn't wish one of them on my worst enemy. I know we've talked about it before, but I'd like to ask you one more time to spread my ashes near the Peaks of Otter. I don't think by law you're allowed to do such a thing, but I'm sure it happens all the time.

Your dad wants his ashes spread up there, too, when *his* time comes, so if it's not too much to ask, please take us in opposite directions. By the lake or back in the campground where we used to, um, watch the deer is fine. I still can't figure out how those apple slices kept *falling* out of our car. I'm sure that happens all the time, too.

Even with the tumor, I still have my memories. I probably spend far too much time with them, but in them I see you, unlike the present. I love you nonetheless, and hope you can forgive me for all the things I've done wrong. I'm sure the list is even longer than I realize, but none of us is perfect, including you. Why you insist on keeping me at arm's length I'm not sure I fully understand, but I accept you for who you are, and I always will.

The brain is a battlefield where we trade victories and losses with ourselves. My fight is all but over, but my illness has taught me to never raise the white flag of surrender. I hope that you will do the same. Never give up on your dreams, especially the one of a cabin in the mountains. Yes, I still remember you telling me about that.

If you make it there in this life, I wish the two of you and your dogs all the happiness in the world and limitless mornings of breathing in the clean air. But if you don't make it there until the afterlife, maybe you'd let me take the dogs for a walk every once in a while to give you two the chance to make up for all the lost time. No pressure.

Missing you and hoping you make it happen.

Your crazy, loving mother."

Rebeca pressed STOP when María Luisa reached for the headphones.

07:45 h

A furgoneta bucketed past La Rinconera. Its low beams bounced uselessly off the wet pavement, but they were on for safety's sake in a red-eyed town waking up with a post-fiestas hangover.

The mood inside the apartment was also dreary, but a mentally and physically exhausted Rebeca was seeing things ever so clearly. She took one last look at herself in the mirror and went in search of her mother. She found her holding a thoroughly unenjoyable cup of coffee at the kitchen table, along with María Luisa, who at Sra. Navas's insistence, was having a glass of juice.

"Where's Papá?" Rebeca asked.

"He called Álvaro first thing, and they went downstairs early."

"How's Álvaro taking all of this?" María Luisa asked, pouring a glass for Rebeca, who politely refused it.

"No better than the rest of us, perhaps worse."

"I can't say I'm surprised."

Rebeca shook her head. "Mamá, I don't want it, but thank you anyway."

Sra. Navas put the juice in her hand. "You're drinking it, and that's that. Vitamin C is good for a cold."

"About that," Rebeca said.

"Yes, dear?"

"Can we talk."

"Of course. Let me brush my teeth, and I'll meet you in—"

"My bedroom's fine."

The sisters exchanged glances as Rebeca gulped down the juice. "Why fight it?" she whispered to her sister and set down the glass.

María Luisa nodded and then her eyes followed Rebeca out of the kitchen. *I can see why the boys love to watch her leave*, she admitted, regretting the inappropriateness of the moment. *One day, I'll tell her how great her ass looks.*

Sra. Navas entered Rebeca's untidy room moments later. She noticed the headphones plugged into the recorder, and shut the door.

Continuing to hug her pillow, Rebeca said nothing.

Sra. Navas ignored the mess and sat down. "I don't need to ask if something's wrong."

Rebeca clutched the pillow. "No."

"So tell me *what's* wrong."

"Nothing's *wrong*, but you said my questions and secrets would be safe with you."

"And I promise they will be."

"Even from Papá?"

"Even from Papá," her mother said, squeezing her daughter's legs through the covers.

"Then there's something you need to hear." Rebeca pointed to the headphones.

"I can never hear anything out of those things, and they hurt my ears. If you take them out, can we can listen to it together?"

"I don't want María Luisa to hear."

"Turn it way down, and let's try it that way."

"But—"

"But if it's too loud, I'll put them on and make do."

Rebeca reluctantly unplugged the headphones and, as she had done for her sister, pressed PLAY. She tweaked the volume as Ethan's mother began. When the message ended, she immediately stopped the tape and leaned forward to hug her mother, nearly smothering her with the pillow against her chest.

Tears from her mother's weary eyes dotted the pillow. "I don't know what to say, but thank you for letting me listen to it."

"You're welcome," Rebeca whispered, staring at the crack under her door: no shadow, no slippers, no bare feet.

After a good cry, Sra. Navas sat back.

"I never want to get to a point when we don't talk," Rebeca said. "It would break my heart."

Sra. Navas squeezed Rebeca's legs again. "Me, too," she said as soon as she could speak.

Rebeca's eyes were still on the crack under the door. "But I've done something you may not be very happy about. But I'm not completely sure. Papá would be mortified. Or maybe he wouldn't be."

Sra. Navas smiled faintly, but said nothing.

"I don't really know where to begin, but I've decided to start with this." She buried her face in the pillow and started the tape. There was a much longer silence, and then another message in the same voice began:

"Dear 'Thomas,' In some houses there's a room kept behind invisible velvet ropes that waits for company, a living room in name only with perfectly placed pillows on a spotless sofa and perpetually vacuumed carpeting. Or a bathroom where the good towels hang lintlessly over a basket of tiny soaps next to a bone dry sink. It hurts and saddens me to know that the apartment you never let me see is a dusty, hopeless, lonely warren of these unlivable rooms.

When the psychiatrist recommended that we name Ethan's OCD, I thought she was crazier than I was. But as it turns out, it helps to have—what exactly are you?—some 'thing' at which I can direct my frustration so I don't take it out on Ethan, who's doing a decent job of living with a mental disorder. I know the name Thomas means 'twin,' but I've never been wild about it. Something like 'Dick Checker' or 'Little Fucker' would have been more cathartic, but that's the name Ethan gave you.

So in the spirit of the doctor's orders, let me say this: 'Thomas,' I abhor, abominate, despise, detest, hate, and loathe you with every fiber of my dying being. You have kept my son from me at a time when I need him most, and now I fear it's too late to make amends. You are also ruining his health, his life, and his relationship with his father, and I doubt he would ever be allowed to marry the love of his life because of *you*, you worthless piece of shit. You are an utter embarrassment, and I wish you had never become a part of this family. We have enough problems already.

There, I've said it.

I'm incredibly thankful, however, that you have María Luisa, I mean, Marisa, to lean on. I keep forgetting that she prefers the diminutive of her given name. Give the *marisabidilla* (know-it-all) a huge hug from me the next time you see her.

It must be so hard on her to know that Ethan is secretly head over heels in love with her sister. But since his first day at El Instituto, he's done nothing but talk about Rebeca. 'Cascalina' is a cute nickname for a girl who loves to *cascar* (chatter); I think the shortened form, Lina, is even cuter.

By the way, don't forget to wash your cardigan sweater. How odd that the Spanish word for it is *rebeca*. But I guess it's a good thing; that way, she's always with you. Him.

Sometimes, this imaginary person thing, or whatever you call it, is so confusing.

How sad that her father is so stubborn and closed minded about mental illness, but for now, I think it's better he doesn't know about you. Fight that battle only if you have to. But from what Ethan told me, you may never have to since Rebeca and Álvaro are getting married.

I know a churro is something like a coiled doughnut, but Ethan said the word also means 'botched job.' Maybe when Álvaro was younger, 'Churro' was a cute nickname for him, but now that he's older and a so-so bullfighter, I don't think it's cute at all.

But enough about them.

This sick, stupid gal has spent a lot of time watching the drapes fade in doctors' offices and hospitals lately. It's given me a lot of time to think about what I was going to say to you. After a lot of scribbling, scratching, flipping through the dictionary, and such, this is what I've come up with. I could have said more, or less, but I'm so aware now that time is short. Since you're a personality and not a person, I've decided not to tinker with it obsessively.

From one obsessive-compulsive to another—I know *you're* a full-blown disorder, and *I* just have tendencies—I leave you with the following quote that I fussed with during an especially depressing stay in the hospital. It's quite a paragraph, if I do say so myself, and as you know, I'm not one to toot my own horn. So for what it's worth, here goes:

We are at war with ourselves. The conflict is as wide as the battlefield's synapses are narrow. The lucky ones clearly see the door that leads to peace, limp toward it, and throw it open. Some stagger forward, bleary-eyed, and nudge it open just enough. Others drag themselves aimlessly through the misery until they bang into it and beat their heads ignorantly against it their entire lives. Many collapse on the way or lie hopelessly bruised and broken on the threshold. But the ones who suffer greatest are those who know the door is open and can't help rattling the knob.

Not Hemingway, but not too shabby, right? But I guess I'll never know what you think, not that I even care, you little fucker. Go back to your checking, rattling, straightening, adjusting, finessing, rubbing, tapping, peekabooing, and all the other goddamned games you play.

Hating you still,

Sandra

P.S. Your father still harps on your breaking that doorknob. He doesn't understand *you* either."

"There's nothing else on either side," Rebeca said and stopped the tape. For several minutes the only sound in the suddenly chilly room was the squeak of the bedsprings as she rocked back and forth. The motion was soothing, and it gave her something to do, but María Luisa wasn't going to wait outside forever. "Come in," Rebeca said.

The door creaked open, and her sister slouched into the room, holding her slippers in one hand and the sack in the other. She sat down beside her mother.

"How much could you hear?" Rebeca asked.

"All of it."

"That's what I thought. It was hard to listen to, wasn't it?"

María Luisa nodded. "But I wasn't surprised."

"No, 'Marisa,' I'm sure you weren't. Did you have any idea, Mamá?"

Sra. Navas finally broke her silence. "About María Luisa preferring to be called by her nickname? Of course, but I don't care for it."

"No. About Ethan's OCD?"

"My mother's intuition is usually pretty good," she said, smiling at Rebeca, who stopped rocking.

"What about his being 'secretly head over heels in love' with me?"

"My answer's the same."

"What's Álvaro going to say?" María Luisa asked, conflicted.

"It doesn't matter."

"Why not?"

"Because I finally got the courage and broke up with him yesterday morning."

"Why the hell did you break up with—"

"What really happened last night, Marisa?" Rebeca interrupted, changing the subject with no real intention of dodging the question.

"Why the hell did you break—"

"I'll tell you *after* you tell me what really happened last night."

"María Luisa, Marisa, tell your sister what happened. We'd both like to know."

"None of you understood that I've always preferred my nickname," María Luisa said; "he did. Do you know what it was like to have someone who actually listened to me?" She fought back tears.

Rebeca was calm. "Marisa, please tell me what happened. He must have talked to you during the lucid interval, while I was in the bathroom."

Marisa collected herself. "I know each of you has seen what's inside this," she said, rubbing the sack, "but I wasn't sure what he was going to do when I left him in the antique shop. He had been so conflicted, and now that you've listened to both messages, it's obvious why. And as time got shorter and shorter, his anxiety got worse and worse. He really struggled but couldn't say anything, especially in front of Papá, that stubborn—"

"Not the time, my dear."

"It was a perfect storm."

"What do you mean?" Rebeca asked.

"Little things, insignificant drops that you and I couldn't have cared less about, puddled one by one into a pool so huge that it burst the dam."

Rebeca frowned. "Are you talking about that bully selling bracelets?"

"No, though he would have preferred to avoid that hoodlum. I'm glad that *gamberro* got what he deserved."

"Where did you hear that?" Rebeca asked.

"From you," Marisa said, "when you were on the phone with Paloma: the guy she saw bleeding."

Resisting the urge to raise her voice, Rebeca stared at the recorder. "We were talking about Álvaro. Churro. He fought in the novillada yesterday. Paloma was there and wanted to let me know he got knocked into the barrera and banged his chin."

"Is he okay?" Sra. Navas asked.

Rebeca nodded. "Paloma said he kept pressing his luck with the bull. I think he was trying to win me back."

"You weren't even there," Marisa said.

"No, but he didn't know that. I kept telling him to give up the bulls, but they're his obsession."

"So are you," Marisa added.

"That's not my problem anymore. I don't love him, and really never did, I don't think. Ethan has—had always been the one." Her eyes filled with tears. "Marisa, what did he tell you in the hospital?"

Marisa sighed. "What started all of it was the button on his back pocket. It came off when he was putting away his money. Money was a problem for him, but not in the way you might think. Yes, he was running low, but he wasn't out; he always kept a bit for an emergency tucked away. And he had a credit card. What you need to understand is that sometimes he got to a point when he became so overwhelmed by things that *we* would never even give a moment's thought to— paying a credit card bill, getting into a wallet, putting away a wallet."

Rebeca wiped her eyes. "*Pobrecito.*"

"And when the button came off," Marisa continued, "there was a little piece of thread that came off with it. Anyone else would have tossed it on the floor, but he sat it on the counter for later." Her voice weakened. "Sometimes, even I couldn't fathom all he went through, although he had been telling me about it for years."

Sra. Navas stroked Marisa's hair. "It's okay, hija."

"Keep in mind that when things went wrong with putting away his money, he was all but done for. He just stood there, staring outside, trying to let the moment pass. But it didn't, and then he found a hole in his pocket. Drop by drop, he was drowning. When he saw his reflection in the window, he saw the face he made when 'Thomas' was taking over; it reminded me of that strange smile you see on Greek statues. Anyway, he couldn't go through his 'normal' routine because he knew the saleswoman and you, Mamá, were friends. He was afraid she'd notice his behavior and tell you his secret. So he bolted. He tripped on his way out, the sack hit something, and then he remembered the thread. Whenever he remembered that he had forgotten something, he had to start his entire routine over. The same thing happened when his routine got interrupted. It's one of the reasons the constant phone calls from his mother were so hard on him."

"I can hardly imagine," Sra. Navas said.

Marisa's eyes dropped. "The moment I left to find Paloma, things went straight to Hell, leading to what happened at the bus stop."

"What *did* happen there?" Rebeca asked.

"He had a chance to go through his routine, but if you knew how much he absolutely hated going through all that and how much he hated himself for having to go through it, you wouldn't be surprised that he backed away from his reflection."

"And onto the curb."

"And slipped. When his mother died, he had a hard time getting a lot done. Usually, he would have checked every inch of each stitch of his clothing, fixed all the loose buttons, and such. Those shoes would have gotten re-soled, but . . ."

"But they didn't, and he's gone."

The words hung on the silence that fell on the room. The women sat motionless, their minds wandering to regrets: Sra. Navas, for not saying something; Rebeca, for not saying anything; Marisa, for saying too much.

Marisa broke the silence. "And now *you* owe *me* an explanation," Marisa reminded Rebeca.

"Are you sure you want to hear it."

"Why wouldn't I want to hear it?"

"Because you were in love with him."

Marisa glanced at her mother. "And?"

"And you kept throwing yourself at him, but he turned you down," Rebeca said.

The softer, gentler María Luisa bristled, and a taste of her acidity returned. "Listen here, you skinny, little witch—"

"I'm not going to tell you anything if you call me names. I don't *have* to tell you anything."

Marisa's acid tongue turned quite sour. "Call you names? 'Witch' is nothing. How about cock tease?"

"I'm not a cock tease," Rebeca said.

"Think what you want, but you have—had a great guy who adored you, but you gave him nothing. Nothing but blue balls."

"I didn't love Álvaro," Rebeca said flatly.

"Then what the hell have you been doing for all these years?"

"Trying to find the courage to—"

Marisa's eyes widened. "To do what?"

"To stop listening to what everyone tells me I'm supposed to do and supposed to want to do."

"And?"

"And I finally stopped listening to everyone," Rebeca said without the slightest hint of guilt.

"So what does that mean?" Marisa asked, getting angry. "You were never going to move out?"

"No."

"Then where were you going to go?"

"With Ethan *and* Thomas."

"What the hell is she talking about, Mamá?" Marisa asked, trying to keep her voice down.

Sra. Navas squeezed her older daughter's leg through her bathrobe. "She was in love with him and had been for a very long time."

"But she's had a serious boyfriend since she's known him. It's just *amazing* how all the guys head for Rebeca's locked hole."

"My hole's not locked anymore," Rebeca said as tears streamed down her face.

"If you're telling me that Álvaro got pity sex before you dumped him, then you aren't a cock tease, you're a slut."

"Calm down, María Luisa. Your sister isn't loose, far from it. And you're not listening. Is she, Rebeca?"

"You know?"

Sra. Navas stared at Rebeca's untouched bottle of cough syrup. "I told both of you that not everything needed to be said, but now you might as well put all your cards on the table."

"Well? Get on with it already."

"While you and Mamá were gone to the BurgoCentro, I put on that bra and panties that were lying on the bed when Ethan walked in on me all those years ago. You didn't think my towel dropped by accident that day, did you?"

"You bitch."

"Remember you said you wanted to know. So I made myself feel pretty for the first time in a very long time, maybe ever, and then knocked on his door. He was packing his suitcases, trying to fit all the stuff he'd bought. Shopping bags were everywhere. I could tell that something was wrong. *I* killed two birds with one stone."

"You slept with him?"

"No, we talked for a while. Time got away from me a bit."

"So you didn't sleep with him?"

Rebeca was slow to answer: "No."

"You're driving me crazy," Marisa said, throwing up her arms.

Sra. Navas's face flushed. "Rebeca, tell her."

Rebeca's face was as red as her mother's. "He came in my mouth."

"He fucked your mouth?"

"There was no fucking," Rebeca said, grabbing the cough syrup as her eyes teared. "I guess I had a reaction to Paloma's spicy pipas and the hot sauce he uses."

Marisa hurled her slippers at Rebeca and stormed out of the room with the sack, slamming the door. As she pounded down the hall toward the front bedroom, the glass doorknob inside the gift box bounced on its bed of tissue paper.

EPILOGUE

Virginia's Blue Ridge Mountains
Four autumns later

The bumper sticker had read VIRGINIA IS FOR LOVERS.

'Low-vers' of what? Rebeca asked herself, white-knuckling the steering wheel up State Route 43. *Certainly not this road.*

Marveling at the old growth forest ablaze with vivid shades of red, yellow, and orange, Marisa found nothing not to love.

"The scenery is *precioso*," Rebeca said, "but even in low gear, the car's struggling. And I'm getting carsick."

"The twists and turns don't bother me," Marisa said absently.

"You're not the one driving."

"Let me take a turn, then. I'd love to drive an automatic."

Rebeca shook her head. "You don't have an international permit."

"Who's going to know?"

Rebeca adjusted the rearview mirror. "Didn't you see that policía when we entered Je-fer-son Na-she-own-al Fo-rest?" She had been working hard on her English pronunciation.

"No," Marisa said, recalling the sign but not the policeman, "but unless he's psychic, he'll never know."

Rebeca's eyes returned to the road ahead. "He won't, but why chance it?"

"It's your call, but—"

"What's that funky odor?"

"Overheated brakes," Marisa said. She slid the climate control to recirculated air.

"I've barely touched the pedal, so it must be the cars going down the mountain." Rebeca wiped the sweat off her palms and re-gripped the wheel. "If we go back this way, remind me to pump the brakes."

A few tortuous minutes later, the strain on the engine eased as they topped the valley between the three mountains that form the Peaks of Otter. A rocky creek trickled out of the dormant rhododendrons and mountain laurel lining the road and flowed lazily along Marisa's side of the car.

Rebeca struggled to stay in the moment, her mind musing upon something she had been told in the days immediately following Ethan's death. Her eyes wandered to the creek bed.

She could picture herself standing there in the cold water—blue jeans rolled up to her knees, flirty scarf tied around her waist, moss green bra dangling from her fingertip, rock-hard nipples poking through her wet tank top. "I'm glad we left the dogs at the cabin, but it's nothing they haven't seen before," she could hear herself teasing, leading Ethan by the hand to a nook of boulders—

"Careful," Marisa interrupted gently, pointing.

The wistful daydream melted into the asphalt. As Rebeca's eyes came into focus, they set upon a white-tailed doe and fawn moseying out of the campground. She inched the car forward and stopped to watch the pair browse near the roadside.

"This place is amazing," Marisa whispered.

Rebeca nodded, and the sisters sat in awed silence until a line of cars grew behind them. "We better go," she said, glancing in the mirror. She tickled the accelerator, and the deer bound off toward the lake, visible through the balding trees.

The road rolled toward the bottom of the valley and then reached its northern end at the Blue Ridge Parkway, which wound to the east and to the west, toward Roanoke. With a heavy heart, Rebeca read the sign: *Ro-ah-noke is where Ethan used to buy tomate frito to make pisto.* Short of the intersection, she pulled off to let carfuls of leaf lookers pass, and then mashed the brake.

To the left, poked Sharp Top. To the right, lay Abbott Lake, and in its reflection, Flat Top, the highest of the three mountains. Straight ahead, the fuzzy treetops of Harkening Hill tickled the clear blue sky, and at its base, the Visitor Center welcomed them forward.

"I need to pee," Rebeca said softly, eyeing the nearly full parking area. She carefully crossed the intersection, pulled into a spot near a loop trail, and turned off the car. "I wouldn't mind taking a walk later."

Marisa nodded.

"The keys are in the ignition, but no joy rides."

"I promise not to touch a thing," Marisa whispered. Accustomed to life in Madrid's trendy suburbs, she locked the doors after Rebeca scooted off to the restroom. A dozen visitors came and went before her sister returned, smiling.

"Sorry for the delay," Rebeca said, "but the trail actually starts in back. And I had to ask directions to the spot."

Marisa eased herself out of the car. "How far are we from it?"

"The ranger said that Por-tare's Moun-tane O-ber-luke is four miles in that direction. How far is that in kilometers?"

"Almost seven; not far, but far enough. I better pee, too." She glanced into the back seat.

"Go pee, then," Rebeca said. "When you're done, take a look at that trail. There's no hurry."

After a considerable delay, Marisa ambled back. "So what's the plan?"

"To find the spot where Ethan scattered his mother's ashes and to—"

"I'm talking about the big picture. How long do you intend to stay with Ethan's father?"

"I haven't really decided," Rebeca admitted, "but when you go home next week, I won't be going with you."

"What will you do, then?"

"Mis-ter Cle-mens—"

"He asked us to call him Oliver."

"O-li-ver offered to help in whatever way he could."

Marisa frowned. "What does that mean?"

"It means that he could help me apply for a *visado de estudiante*."

"Is that what you want to do? Study in Estados Unidos?" Marisa asked, coaxing herself into the car.

Rebeca slipped into the car and started it. "We've talked about it, but I'm not sure the timing is right."

Marisa understood. "Of course."

"And what about you?"

"I've thought about studying to become a *psicóloga*."

"Mercedes would have been proud of you, God rest her soul."

"I think so, too," Marisa said, not even tempted to cross herself.

"But going to university is expensive."

"*Muy.*"

"Whatever I do, there's *no way* I can keep working with Papá. Even part time."

"I do give you credit for trying," Rebeca said. "I'm amazed you've lasted this long."

Marisa appreciated the comment. "I don't blame him for what happened, but his dumbass comments made things *so* much worse for Ethan. I can't forgive him for that." She helped Rebeca watch as she backed out. "Don't you think Papá robbed you of your happiness, in some way?"

"I think each of us made mistakes," she said, pulling onto the Parkway, heading west. "No one's perfect. Well, almost no one." She adjusted the rearview mirror again. "Look who just woke up," she said with a proud smile as the preschooler buckled into his safety seat batted his blue eyes awake.

Of all Rebeca's mistakes, providing Ethan release with the most intimate kiss wasn't one of them. And afterward, she had led him to her bedroom, bared her heart to him, and trembled as he confessed his feelings to her. And after their hands had explored and their lips had kissed and whispered sweet plans for the future, their bodies had shared the most intimate gift, quivering as one with nothing between her flesh and his. It was the shared exhalation of deep breaths held for much too long—the wind that had filled their sails and started to push them on a lifelong journey together.

But wind is fickle, and life is precarious.

FIN

About the Author

Tony Houck's burning enthusiasm for Spanish language and culture was sparked by a two-week tour of Spain during high school. Thirty years later, this family man and severe obsessive-compulsive is still bitten by the bug to travel and explore. Set in the Spanish town where he lived, studied, ate tripe, ran with the bulls, and got his heart broken, *The Precariousness of Done* is his first novel.